**Look what people are saying about
these talented auth**

"*My Favorite Mist*   s
gift for weav   romance
that readers find impossible to put down."
—*WordWeaving.com*

"*This* is a sexy book."
—*Romance Reading Room* on *My Favorite Mistake*

Jennifer
LaBrecque

"LaBrecque writes her characters to jump off the pages."
—*The Romance Reader*

"A vividly emotional and erotic tale about
two wonderfully complex characters,
spiced liberally with humor."
—*Romantic Times BOOKclub*

Rhonda
Nelson

"Quirky, irreverent and laugh-out-loud hilarious,
Rhonda Nelson speaks my language!"
—*New York Times* bestselling author Vicki Lewis Thompson

"A witty sensual tale, featuring a completely
unforgettable pair of lovers. Very, very hot!"
—*Romantic Times BOOKclub*

ABOUT THE AUTHORS

Bestselling author *Stephanie Bond* married a guy she swore she'd never date—a younger man who worked for the same company she did! But fifteen years later she thinks things have worked out rather nicely. Stephanie is living happily ever after with her wholly unsuitable and completely incredible guy in midtown Atlanta. Visit Stephanie and find out more about her Harlequin novels at www.stephaniebond.com.

While award-winning author *Jennifer LaBrecque* would be the last person to say she was married to a geek (husbands can be so sensitive about things like that), she firmly believes you should never say "never." Jennifer lives in suburban Atlanta with one husband (not a geek, no, really), one daughter, two cats, two greyhounds and a Chihuahua who runs the whole show. She'd love you to visit her at www.jenniferlabrecque.com.

Bestselling author *Rhonda Nelson* loves writing hot romantic comedy. In addition to a writing career she has a husband, two adorable kids, a black Lab and a beautiful bichon frise who dogs her every step and who frequently cocks his head in utter bewilderment at her. (Rhonda often affects people like this.) She and her family make their chaotic but happy home in a small town in northern Alabama. She tries to see the best in everybody and wouldn't mind at all if her husband decided to moonlight as a used car salesman, particularly if he could put her behind the wheel of a vintage Corvette.

3 Guys You'll Never Date

Stephanie Bond

Jennifer LaBrecque

Rhonda Nelson

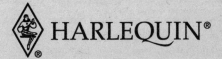

HARLEQUIN®

TORONTO • NEW YORK • LONDON
AMSTERDAM • PARIS • SYDNEY • HAMBURG
STOCKHOLM • ATHENS • TOKYO • MILAN • MADRID
PRAGUE • WARSAW • BUDAPEST • AUCKLAND

ISBN-13: 978-0-373-83718-2
ISBN-10:   0-373-83718-6

3 GUYS YOU'LL NEVER DATE

Copyright © 2006 by Harlequin Books S.A.

The publisher acknowledges the copyright holders
of the individual works as follows:

YOU CAN LEAVE YOUR HARD HAT ON
Copyright © 2006 by Stephanie Bond, Inc.

THE TOTAL PACKAGE
Copyright © 2006 by Jennifer LaBrecque.

HER HERO?
Copyright © 2006 by Rhonda Nelson.

This edition published by arrangement with Harlequin Books S.A.

® and TM are trademarks of the publisher. Trademarks indicated with
® are registered in the United States Patent and Trademark Office, the
Canadian Trade Marks Office and in other countries.

www.eHarlequin.com

Printed in U.S.A.

CONTENTS

The three authors would like to dedicate this book to the memory of Nana, who introduced the love of romance novels to her granddaughter, Brenda Chin, who launched all of our writing careers.

YOU CAN LEAVE
YOUR HARD HAT ON

Stephanie Bond

PROLOGUE

"SO THE QUESTION IS," Samantha Stone said, arching her eyebrows at her long-distance best friends Abby Vandiver and Carley DeLuna, "where *are* all the good men?"

The women each maintained hectic schedules yet never missed a quarterly lunch and shopping date in Manhattan, where their respective careers took them on occasion.

Sam ran a finger over the line sketch she'd doodled—on a cocktail napkin—of her upcoming architectural project, which was expected to cement her reputation. "I mean, here we are, three fabulous, successful women in our early thirties, and we're single." Tucking a strand of long blond hair behind her ear, she frowned. "I could understand if we all lived in the same city—but it's the same story in Dallas, D.C. and Charlotte. I think what we're witnessing is a nationwide shortage of marriageable men."

Abby Vandiver, a D.C. marketing wunderkind, made a derisive noise, her silvery-gray eyes flashing. "The problem is that smart, self-made women are too threatening to men's fragile egos. Trust me—my ex-husband is a prime example. Big-boobed waitresses are much easier to deal with than a woman who might take your job." The frustration on her face was clear—she could make over a so-so product and turn it into an overnight sensation, but she hadn't been able to find a man who didn't want to make *her* over.

Carley DeLuna nodded, her brown curls bobbing, her dark eyes solemn beneath the brim of a pale-blue Parisian couture hat. Over the past few years, Carley had turned her unassuming upscale vintage clothing store in Charlotte into *the* East Coast source for A-list celebrities. "Think about it—even the guys we knew at Wharton dated women who were beneath them on the economic food chain."

Abby nodded. "So if we're near the top of that food chain, where does that leave us?"

"Lonely," Carley said, her voice wistful. Of their threesome, she had always been the romantic. She toyed with the Ford Thunderbird convertible brochure lying next to her plate. "It's enough to make me think twice about buying my new car. Maybe it's too…pretentious."

"Are you kidding me?" Abby said. "You'll look terrific sitting behind the wheel of that car. Men don't mind announcing their success, and neither should we."

"Right." Samantha sipped from her second glass of wine—or was it her third? The two empty bottles of merlot on the table might explain their philosophical state of mind. "And personally, I'd rather be lonely than settle for a man who isn't my equal on every level."

"Hear, hear," Abby said. "I've worked so hard to break the glass ceiling at my company—I refuse to downplay my success in order to find romance."

"I feel the same way," Carley said. "I couldn't be happy with someone who doesn't have the same drive that I have." Then she frowned. "Unfortunately, the only men who ask me out still live with their mothers."

Abby and Samantha groaned in sympathy.

"I'm on the radar of every loser in D.C.," Abby said. "I meet a cute guy on the train, and, inevitably, he's barely employed."

"*If* he's employed," Samantha said. "I've dated more guys who are 'between jobs' than I care to remember. A couple of them even asked me to help them *find* jobs."

"Good grief," Abby said. "Call me shallow, but I'm a successful woman, and I think I deserve to have a successful man in my life."

"But not just successful," Samantha offered dreamily. "Someone who makes those long hours at the office worthwhile…who likes adventure…who pushes me out of my comfort zone…"

"You're twirling your hair," Carley chided.

Abby harrumphed. "And you're describing someone who, to my knowledge, doesn't exist."

"God, I hope that isn't true," Sam said, stopping mid-twirl to tuck her hair back, keeping with her polished public image.

Carley tapped her finger on the car brochure. "Maybe we need to be more…selective. You know—raise our standards."

"Amen," Abby said. "And stick to them. Hold out for a man who is worthy of our fabulousness."

"You're right," Sam said, perking up. "After all, there must be three quality men out there...*somewhere*."

"All we need is one in Dallas, one in D.C. and one in Charlotte," Carley said with a laugh.

"It's going to be like finding a needle in a haystack," mused Abby the cynic. "Think it's possible?"

"Absolutely," Carley insisted.

"A pact," Samantha said, raising her glass. "No more dating unsuitable guys."

"No freaks," Carley said, raising her glass.

"No geeks," Abby said, raising hers.

"No bartenders," chimed in Samantha.

"No janitors," Carley added.

"No ditch-diggers," Samantha said.

"No unemployed actors, musicians or artists," Abby added.

"And no used-car salesmen," rounded out Carley.

"Agreed," Samantha said, clinking her glass against theirs, then glanced at her watch. "Oh, sorry, girls—I've got to go or I'll miss my flight. How about if we compare notes in three months?" They checked their PDAs and set a tentative date for their next rendezvous, to coincide with Abby's return to Manhattan for a seminar.

"Good luck with your plans to build the Carlyle Library," Abby said to Samantha in between farewell hugs.

"Thanks. Good luck with your next makeover project. And Carley, I'll look for one of your gowns on the red carpet of the Academy Awards."

Carley dimpled. "Thanks."

"And don't forget our pact," Samantha said as she backed away from the table. "No matter how lonely we get or how tempted we are, we have to keep reminding ourselves that there are certain kinds of guys that women should never date." She grinned. "I have a good feeling about this."

"Me, too," Abby said.

"And me," Carley agreed. "In fact, I'll wager that the next time we get together, we'll be talking about the rich, worldly, glamorous men in our lives!"

CHAPTER ONE

"LADIES AND GENTLEMEN, we're making our final approach into Dallas. At this time, please stow your tray tables and return your seats to their upright position. And remember, there are some guys that you should never date."

Samantha Stone's eyes popped open and she straightened in her window seat. As the rest of the flight announcement floated away, she realized that in her dream state she had projected her own thoughts through the PA system. She'd definitely had too much wine with the girls.

Next to her, a young couple sat with their shoulders and heads close, poring over brochures of Hawaii—their obvious destination after connecting in Dallas. Their excitement and love for each other overflowed in every glance, every gesture. They could barely keep their hands off each other.

Sam's heart squeezed with an unidentifiable emotion—envy? The way the young man's fingers mirrored the young woman's, pressing intimately before intertwining, pinged a memory chord. Unbidden, a set of hooded green eyes rose in her mind—he had laced their hands over her head as he had settled his body over hers, with the most intense eye contact and the most complete connection that she had ever experienced with a man.

Sam blinked. Only Teague Brownlee hadn't been a man—he'd been a handsome rebel boy with raging hormones and a desire to bed a girl way out of his league. They'd shared a one-night stand the night of graduation…the culmination of four years of flirtatious looks across the crowded halls of their high school from the safe confines of their respective cliques—hers the most popular, his the most notorious.

She willed away the distant memory, as she had a thousand times before, but it stubbornly lingered. Forgetting Teague Brownlee had become an automatic reflex after she had left Gypsum, a suburb of Dallas, to study architecture at Georgia Tech in Atlanta. She had been single-minded, determined to get her degree in record time while maintaining top honors.

That forbidden night with Teague had crept into her thoughts often in those days, usually at night when she'd pulsed with homesickness and loneliness. But the desire to be in his arms had been overridden by her desire to succeed, to prove her mettle to her successful father, to make her mark in what was still primarily a man's industry. Being involved with someone like Teague, a guy with no ambition and no prospects, would only have held her back. Besides, she'd burned that bridge the morning after their illicit night together.

She hadn't thought of Teague in years and blamed the

flashback on the lunch talk with Abby and Carley. Deep down, she wondered if her vehemence in denouncing men who were less driven had something to do with Teague Brownlee. She remembered feeling frustrated and angry that he'd seemed directionless and bound for mediocrity because she'd thought he could do better for himself…that they might have had more than one night together if he hadn't been willing to settle for a small life in the small town of Gypsum. She idly wondered what had become of him and decided that he was doing something with his hands or working in one of Gypsum's factories, probably married to a pretty Gypsum girl, the two of them raising a gaggle of wild Gypsum kids.

Through the small rectangular window the Dallas skyline came into view. Fondness swelled Sam's chest. She knew each building by its shape and height, knew the architect's name and the approximate year it had been erected. Someday she hoped that her own unique structures would pierce the skyline, that the name Samantha Stone would be synonymous with progressive architecture and an era of new growth for the city.

The young woman next to her laughed, touching her boyfriend's face. They were oblivious to her. Sam shifted slightly in her seat to give them more room, more privacy…and to distance herself from their intimacy.

When she was their age, she was contemplating postgraduate work at Wharton, where she would eventually meet Abby and Carley. She had taken herself so seriously, always thinking that there would be time for a relationship after she finished school, after she was situated in a good career path.

But instead of slowing down, her life had only become more hectic. One assignment had melded into another as she tried to prove herself to the partners in the architecture firm where she worked. There hadn't been time to foster a romantic attachment, and the few men she had dated, frankly, hadn't been worth the trouble. She wanted a man who appreciated her intellect instead of being threatened by it, yet who still could make her feel like a woman. When she'd turned thirty-one a few months ago, she had felt a little desperate around the edges with no significant other and no significant work accomplishments in the foreseeable future.

And then the Carlyle Library project had materialized.

Sam closed her eyes briefly, smiling as she imagined the finished structure. Once completed, the private, three-story corporate library would be her first signature building. Competition for the design on the Carlyle Library had been fierce, and the partners in her firm had been jubilant when Sam had won the project. No one, however, had been more thrilled than she, and she wasn't about to mess up this chance of a lifetime. Her first hurdle was to manage the initial phase of the job—excavation of the site. Although the board of directors had commended her innovative design, they had expressed doubts about its viability on the sloping site that had been chosen.

The thrill of telling her father, a wildly successful developer with investments in every corner of Texas, that she'd been awarded the project had diminished when he had expressed similar concerns about her design. The frown of Packard Stone's doubt was etched into her brain. The hurt that had sliced through her chest at his skepticism had given way to disappointment, then determination. It was how her father had raised her, after all. She intended to overcome the engineering obstacles with a new concept for building retaining walls. If she could successfully manage the excavation on time—thirty days—and on budget, she would receive a green light on the entire project. If not, her career-making landmark would perish before it even got off the ground.

But she would not allow that to happen.

When they deplaned, Sam watched the young couple until they disappeared into the crowd, their hands clasped like a vise. A pang of longing hit her with the force of a blow to the stomach, stopping her midstride, disorienting her. Sam stood still for a moment as people walked all around her, brushing past as they hurried to meet their parties. Everyone seemed to be hurrying to meet someone…everyone except her. The noises around her suddenly seemed muffled, as if she were standing in a vacuum. She hadn't felt so acutely alone since the day her mother had died, when Sam was seven years old.

The world had fallen away from her that day, leaving her cold and scared and wondering if anyone would ever again love her with such intensity. Packard had tried, but he was a salty Texan businessman, inconvenienced by his slip of a daughter. Out of necessity, Sam had learned to be self-reliant, reluctant to let anyone get close enough to make her emotionally dependent.

Sam breathed deeply, and slowly her vital signs returned to normal. Someday soon—perhaps after the Carlyle Library project—she would be more open to a relationship and make an effort to meet men.

Successful men, she reminded herself with a smirk. She hadn't held out for the right man this long only to settle now. An attractive attorney had recently moved into her building, on her floor, and had been making small talk at the elevator. She hadn't felt a chemical reaction between them, but maybe the timing had been wrong.

When she next saw what's-his-name, she promised herself, she would make an effort to strike up a conversation.

Sam glanced at her watch and headed for the airport exit, her stride lengthening. Equipment would be arriving on the library job site today, and the ground would be broken. And even though the foreman she'd hired had assured her that he had things under control, she wanted to stop by the site, just in case. She looked down at her clothing and ruefully conceded that a cream-colored skirt and jacket, yellow silk blouse and pale, lizard-skin pumps weren't exactly job-site attire, but they'd have to do.

She was, after all, the boss.

She gave the taxi driver directions to the job site, then

pulled site maps from her briefcase so the specifications would be fresh in her mind. Within seconds, she was immersed in the world she loved—a world of exact dimensions and tangible materials that would, under her guidance, turn an empty lot of loose dirt into the home for a building that would be a permanent symbol of her success…one that her father and everyone else would have to acknowledge.

"Are you sure this is it?" the cabbie asked.

Sam lifted her head from the maps and surveyed the plot of land dotted with heavy equipment and marked with the sign The Future Home Of The Carlyle Library. "Yes. I should be only a few minutes—can you wait?"

"Sure."

Sam folded the papers and returned them to her briefcase, anticipation hammering in her chest. She alighted onto the curb and inhaled the scent of freshly turned dirt, sighing in satisfaction to see that work had already begun. But as she picked her way across the uneven ground, she was frustrated to see several workers standing around or, worse, sitting down. A couple of card games had broken out on the tailgates of pickup trucks, and more than one worker was sipping on a beer, a blatant work-site violation.

Where was her foreman?

While she stood frowning at the scene before her, catcalls began to sound all around her.

"Woo-hoo, pretty lady, are you lost?"

"Where've you been all my life, darlin'?"

Sam scowled at the men—it wasn't the first time she'd been harassed on a job site. "Where is Mr. Langtry, the foreman?"

Shrugs ensued and many of the men adopted suggestive stances. "I can be anybody you want me to be," one of them shouted, inciting a round of raucous laughter.

Anger sparked in her stomach, but Sam ignored the men and began to make her way toward a section of the site where a deep channel was being dug—a channel that wasn't on the site plans. The ground was soft from recent rains, and she knew she probably looked ridiculous hobbling around in her high heels, but frustration spurred her forward. Chaos and improperly placed ditches this early in the process were not good signs. She shouldered the strap of her briefcase, then cupped her hands like a bullhorn. *"Has anyone seen Mr. Langtry?"*

Unfortunately, the movement threw her off balance. She flailed to regain her footing but failed miserably and tumbled toward the trench being dug. Her pride flashed before her eyes—she only hoped she didn't break something important when she landed at the bottom. At the last second, she had the impression of a yellow hard hat, a bare chest and a pair of muscular arms reaching for her.

When she opened her eyes, she was being held aloft by a man who had been standing in the muddy channel and, judging by the shovel lying nearby, was responsible for most of the dirt that had been moved. Sam's initial emotion was gratitude, although she realized instantly that being rescued by one of the workers would probably be more damaging to her reputation than if she'd wound up at the bottom of the ditch with her skirt over her head.

But when she turned her head to look at the shirtless man who held her, her breath caught in her throat. Denial exploded in her brain, but there was no denying the taunting, impossibly green eyes under the brim of the hard hat. Teague Brownlee.

CHAPTER TWO

TEAGUE TOOK A DEEP BREATH and inhaled the enticing scent that had haunted him for over a decade—Spring Blush. He had seen the perfume bottle among Samantha Stone's things when he'd spent the night in her bed. But even though she still wore the same perfume, Samantha had changed. Gone was the fringe of blond bangs that she had pushed back from her face as she'd walked through the halls of their high school. Now her long, pale hair was one length and fashionably straight. And the curves he felt beneath her finely cut suit were fuller, more womanly, than the last time he'd held her.

It had been a magical night, one created by desperation on his part. Samantha Stone had been the only thing in high school that had held his interest. Born into wealth and privilege, Samantha had run with the cool kids and had enjoyed the fruits of her social status and beauty. He, on the other hand, had been born into hardship and had run with the kids spoiling for trouble. With her golden good looks and slender curves dressed in the best clothes that money could buy, Samantha had represented every-thing that Teague couldn't have. And, despite the haughty looks she had cast in his direction, his desire for her had kept him awake too many nights to count.

He'd known that Samantha was headed to college in Atlanta after graduation, so, aware that his window of opportunity to get her attention was closing, he and his buddies had crashed Samantha's graduation party at her father's mansion. She'd been amused by his actions and had not only allowed them to stay but had wound up spending the night with Teague in the guesthouse—an amazing night of sex and intimate pillow talk that was seared into Teague's memory. Sometime between midnight and dawn, he had even started to believe he was in love with her. The next morning, however, Samantha was gone, leaving a note that read "Don't track dirt on my carpet when you leave."

Humiliated to the core, Teague had vowed to himself that one day Samantha Stone would get her comeuppance. In truth, he was only mildly surprised at the identity of the woman in his arms. He'd always known that his and Samantha's paths would cross again—he just hadn't expected her to drop into his life so literally, while he stood ankle-deep in black mud.

If he'd had any doubts that she would recognize him, they were erased by the look of pure mortification—and dismay—on her face. "Teague Brownlee?"

He gave her a flat smile. "Samantha Stone. It's been a while."

She frowned, clearly displeased to see him. "What are you doing here?"

"I'm digging a ditch," he said, stating the obvious. "What are *you* doing here?"

"This is my job site."

He raised his eyebrows. "Yours?"

"That's right. I'm the architect for the library. And for your information, this ditch you're digging isn't on the site plan."

"Really? Then it should be."

She narrowed her eyes. A crowd had begun to gather, with wolf whistles and halfhearted applause.

"Good catch, Teague!"

"Looks like you got your hands full, Teague!"

Teague grinned, enjoying seeing her squirm. His sex hardened as she pushed against his bare chest, her soft fingers and biting nails bringing back vivid memories of the last time she had touched him, had coaxed him to the heights of physical release. Eighteen-year-old hormones were suddenly resurrected and raged through his body. Just like that, he wanted her…and he hated himself for it.

Samantha glared at the jeering workers, then at Teague. "I'd appreciate it if you'd put me down."

Irritation barbed through his chest. "You're welcome for keeping you from breaking your neck. I see you haven't changed."

Samantha glanced at his sweaty, dirty arms, then arched a haughty eyebrow. "I could say the same thing."

He clenched his jaw—Samantha still knew his soft-tissue points. The moment was oddly reminiscent of the last time they'd been together—he'd been too dirty for her then, too. Teague tightened his grip on her, not caring that he was soiling her designer suit, then brought his mouth close to her ear. "Give me one good reason why I shouldn't drop your ungrateful behind in the mud."

Cheers and jeers continued to sound around them. Samantha narrowed her blue eyes. "Because I'm your boss and if you value your job, you'll behave accordingly."

Teague pursed his mouth and nodded slowly. "Okay." Then he opened his arms and let her fall.

She landed with a splat in six inches of goo. From her mouth came a startled cry of disbelief, her eyes wide as the mud enveloped her.

The workers erupted in screams of laughter, and Teague experienced a flash of remorse—she looked like a drowned kitten. He leaned over and extended his hand, but Samantha slapped it away.

"Don't touch me!" Seeing the way she recoiled from him, his remorse vanished. He crossed his arms to enjoy the show.

She flailed like a wounded animal as she rescued her briefcase and pushed herself up from the muck with a great sucking noise. She stood, mud-soaked from the waist down, the hem of her skirt dragging from the weight of the wetness that had soaked through the fabric, molding it to her shapely backside. She was a pitiful sight, her hair and face splattered, but her chin was high with defiance. The top of the ditch met her shoulder-level. She gave him a lethal glare, then tossed her briefcase up. A couple of grinning men standing above them moved to extend their hands.

"Get out of my way," she yelled, then proceeded to hoist herself up with her arms and lift herself out of the ditch with an impressive show of strength—and leg. Between the wiggle of her behind, the sight of her toned thighs, and the flash of brown leopard-print panties, Teague had to fist his hands to keep from reaching for her.

When she finally stood above him, her generous chest rose and fell from exertion and, he suspected, anger. "May I have my shoes, please?" she asked in a regal voice.

Teague pondered her request but conceded that she'd have a hard time getting home without shoes. He leaned over and fished her high heels out of the mud, turned them over until the goop stopped running out of them, then reached up to set them on the ground. She slipped her stocking feet inside the shoes, picked up her brief-case, then latched on to him with blazing blue eyes. "You. Are. Fired."

CHAPTER THREE

A few chuckles and guffaws sounded around them as her words vibrated in the air.

Chest heaving, Sam stared down at the unwelcome blast from her past as white-hot anger whipped through her. As if the shock of seeing Teague again wasn't enough, the nerve of the man to humiliate her in front of everyone on the job site was unforgivable. She'd had no choice but to fire him.

He stood looking up at her, his green eyes mocking beneath his hard hat. He was still tall and lean, but his body had filled in with solid muscle. His broad, bare chest was slick with perspiration, highlighting a long, angry scar on his shoulder and flattening the dark hair that converged over the planes of his stomach and disappeared into the waistband of his raggedy, faded jeans.

She held her breath, waiting for him to respond. Moving with languid indifference, he reached over to pick up the shovel he'd dropped, propped it on his thick shoulder, then touched his hand to his hard hat. "No offense, ma'am, but you can't fire me."

She lifted her chin. "Yes, I can."

"No, you can't," he countered quietly. "Because I quit."

Soft laughter sounded around them as he climbed out of the trench with the ease of an athlete. He walked by her without a sideways glance, so close that she could feel the heat rolling off his half-naked body. He whistled and out of nowhere a chocolate-colored Labrador appeared and fell into step next to him as he strode toward a black king cab pickup.

Sam straightened her shoulders and addressed the frowning workers standing around. "Now, can anyone tell me where I can find Mr. Langtry?"

Finally a young woman removed her hard hat and stepped forward. "He didn't show up today, ma'am."

Sam nodded curtly. "Thank you. Listen up, everyone. Until Mr. Langtry can be located, I'm in charge. My name is Samantha Stone—I'm the architect for this building and I'll be overseeing the excavation." She scanned the workers, a bit dismayed to see that no one seemed particularly impressed or attentive. Admittedly, though, she probably looked ridiculous covered in mud. She took a deep breath and summoned strength, pointing to the deep, wide channel that Teague had been digging. "I want that ditch filled."

The workers looked at each other, then back to her.

"Beg your pardon, ma'am," one of the workers said, "but Teague said that's where one of the retaining walls should be."

Sam bit the inside of her cheek, then gave the worker a flat smile. "Well, *Teague* was wrong. Fill it in."

She turned and made her way back across the job site with as much dignity as she could muster. Teague's truck was gone, and just the thought of him filled her with fury all over again. What ghastly luck to cross paths with him again on this, the most important project of her career. Tears pressed on the back of her eyes, but she clenched her jaw to keep them at bay. She had vowed never to cry on the job, and she wasn't going to start today.

When she reached the taxi, the driver jumped out. "What happened?"

"I fell."

"I have a tarp in the trunk," he said, then sprang into action. After he spread the blue plastic tarp on the back seat, Sam crawled in, feeling utterly miserable. How had this day gone so badly, so quickly?

Teague Brownlee, that's how.

She leaned her head back on the seat and exhaled. Good grief, where had he come from? The man was like a bolt of lightning, striking without notice and leaving her scorched—again. She still tingled from their encounter and wondered crazily if she had conjured him with her wayward thoughts on the return flight from New York.

She dug her cell phone out of her waterlogged briefcase and dialed the number for Mr. Langtry. When he didn't answer, she dialed her assistant.

"Samantha Stone's office, Price speaking."

"Price, it's Sam," she said, squeezing the bridge of her nose where the pressure of a headache had begun to throb. "I'm back."

"Hi, boss. How was Manhattan?"

"Let's just say I wish I'd stayed there."

"What's up?"

"I just stopped by the Carlyle site, and it's chaos."

"Yikes."

"Don't say anything to anyone," she warned. "The last thing I need is for everyone at the firm to think things have started badly."

"What can I do?"

"My site foreman is missing in action—think you can track him down?"

"I'll give it the old college try."

"His name is Langtry. Gerald Langtry."

"Got it. Where will you be?"

"At my condo." She frowned at her ruined suit and shoes. "I had a little accident at the site."

"Are you okay?"

"Yes, but my Dana Buchman suit and Judith Leiber shoes are in critical condition. I'm going home to shower."

He groaned. "I'll check to see if Manolo makes steel-toed stilettos."

She laughed. "Thanks."

"No problem. Oh, and your father called."

Sam winced. "Did he leave a message?"

"He's coming to town at the end of the month and wants to see you."

Translation: Packard wanted to check out the Carlyle Library job site for himself. Just what she didn't need— someone else questioning her design. "Okay, thanks,

Price. I'll be in the office tomorrow. Call me the minute you find Langtry."

"Will do."

She disconnected the call just as the cab pulled up to her building. The cabbie retrieved her carry-on suitcase from the trunk. She climbed out and handed him the fare and a hefty tip, grimacing at the grit in her shoes that chafed her feet. Hoping she didn't run into any of her neighbors in the eight-story building, she entered the revolving door and practically ran through the lobby, past the concierge and onto one of the elevators. To her chagrin, she left a trail of dried mud behind her.

But when she reached the top floor and the elevator doors opened, the attractive attorney who had just moved in stood waiting. Sam bit back a groan—talk about bad timing. She frantically searched her memory for his name—Stanley? No, Stewart. Stewart Estes.

Stewart blinked at her appearance. "Samantha, what on earth—"

"Long story," she said, sweeping by.

"Maybe you can tell me about it some time," he called.

Remembering her vow to make an effort, she turned and tossed her mud-soaked hair behind her shoulder. "I'd like that."

"I'll call you," he said, smothering a smile as the elevator closed.

She winced. The man probably thought she was some sort of mud-wrestler. She made a dash for her condo and opened the door to a world of soaring white walls, plush white rugs over white epoxy floors, sleek white leather furniture and gleaming stainless steel accessories, the wall of windows facing downtown free of drapes or other clutter. Clean and soothing, just how she liked it.

Sam removed her shoes and picked her way carefully across the entryway and down the hall to her bathroom, where she turned on the shower. A glimpse of herself in the mirror made her gasp in dismay—her face was spotted with dried mud, her pale hair matted. Her clothes and shoes were beyond saving. Damn Teague Brownlee! She withdrew a garbage bag from beneath the sink and peeled off her sodden clothes, stuffing them inside with jerky, angry movements. Even her underwear was ruined.

She stepped into the shower, hoping the water would wash away some of her tension, as well as the grime. But when she closed her eyes to lather her skin and hair, she kept replaying the scene over and over in her head— of Teague catching her, their moment of electric recognition, then his audacity to drop her in the mud in front of everyone *after* she'd told him that it was her job site. Clearly he'd felt threatened by her authority. If she'd been a male architect walking onto that site, things would have ended very differently.

She was still fuming when she toweled off. Men like Teague Brownlee kept chauvinism alive in the building industry.

After slipping into black slacks and a slate-blue button-up blouse, she was compelled to pull her high school yearbook from her bookcase. She bypassed the pictures of herself—her circle of friends were some of the most photographed and popular kids in school—and turned to the senior portraits. Most of the boys had worn formal jackets and tuxes for their portraits, their hair neat and stylish. But Teague stuck out in his battered leather jacket and T-shirt, his hair shaggy, his face lean and rawboned, his eyes full of rebellion.

His family had been large and troublesome, she recalled, and he had lived in a rural area of Gypsum where she'd never been. They'd had nothing in common, yet their gazes had caught often in the halls at school or in the cafeteria. There had been something challenging in his eyes, as if he wasn't impressed by her daddy's money or her brand-new car or her rich friends. And there had been something blatantly sexual in the way he'd looked at her. She'd never been afraid, only…intrigued.

When he and his buddies had crashed her graduation party, she'd been more amused than angry and had given in to the powerful chemistry between them that had never been explored. Dancing had led to kissing and kissing had led to petting and petting had led to the bedroom in the guesthouse. Her party forgotten, they had spent the night together, exploring each other's bodies in what had been a sense-shattering experience for her. Teague had been her first lover, a tidbit that she'd kept to herself.

He'd been an intense, exciting bed partner, in tune with her desires and his own. When their lust had been sated, they had talked about things that were happening in the world and about their dreams. At the time, it had made her feel very philosophical and wise, but the next morning, reality had settled in. Her dreams had centered around success and career, his had centered around family and obligation. Her dreams would take her away from Gypsum. His dreams would likely keep him there.

She had also been embarrassed that after saving herself for so long, she had given her virginity to the most unsuitable man in her proximity. And, admittedly, she had been a little scared by the depth of emotion he had evoked within her—it had made her doubt her life plan, a plan she had already set into motion, a plan that didn't have room for a rough-edged, unpredictable boyfriend. There were times though, when she'd wondered what Teague might have become with the love and support of a strong woman….

Sam sighed and shook her head. It was silly to conjure up fantasies of what might have been—they each had chosen their own path. Such a shame that the man was digging ditches for a living…although wasn't it exactly what she'd expected him to do with his life?

Her cell phone rang, breaking into her nostalgic musings. She connected the call. "Hello?"

"Samantha, hey, it's Price. I found your foreman, Mr. Langtry."

She smiled in relief. "Great."

"Um, not really. He's in Central Hospital with mono."

"Mono?"

"Yeah, says he's going to be out of commission for at least six weeks."

Her shoulders fell and worst-case scenarios ballooned in her mind—missing the excavation deadline, having the project yanked, embarrassing her firm, facing her father.

"But don't panic," Price added quickly. "I have him on the line and he says he can recommend a replacement."

"Okay, put him on."

The phone clicked and a scratchy voice said, "Hello?"

"Mr. Langtry?"

"Yeah, it's me," he said, sounding horrible. "Hello, Miss Stone. I guess your secretary told you I was going to be laid up for a while."

"I'm an executive assistant," Price broke in.

"Yes," Sam said. "I'm sorry to hear about your illness, Mr. Langtry."

"I know I'm leaving you high and dry on your job, Miss Stone."

"Price said you could recommend a replacement."

"Sure can. Name's Brownlee."

She swallowed hard and reached for a table to lean against. "*Teague* Brownlee?"

"You know him?"

She winced. "Yes. I fired him today."

Langtry laughed. "You don't say?"

"Well, actually, he quit."

"You two have a run-in at the site?"

"Something like that."

He laughed again, obviously amused. "Well, I have to be honest with you, Miss Stone—the crew was already unhappy working on a job that they saw as short-term. If you don't have a foreman on the job tomorrow, the crew leaders are liable to take their men to another job. They all like Teague—they'll stay for him. This is a tricky site, and he's the smartest man I know when it comes to excavation."

She bit back a curse. "Surely there must be someone else."

"Not someone who's available on a day's notice. Teague only works when he wants to."

She rolled her eyes at that bit of information, then sighed. "Will you call and talk to him?"

"If he has a phone, I don't know the number. Anytime I want to talk to Teague, I go to the billiards joint on West Avenue called Brass Balls. He's usually hanging out there."

Her mouth tightened. So the man rarely worked and spent most of his time playing pool—at a place called Brass Balls, no less. "Okay, thank you, Mr. Langtry, for the information. I hope you're feeling better soon."

"Good luck, Miss Stone. I know how much is riding on this excavation."

He clicked off, and Price said, "So… What did this Brownlee guy do that you had to fire him?"

She closed her eyes. "I fell into a ditch and he caught me."

"And?"

"And then...he dropped me...in the mud."

Price gasped. "Oh, that's...not funny, Samantha, I swear I'm not laughing. But if it was an accident..."

"He did it on purpose."

"Why?" he sputtered.

"To embarrass me in front of the workers."

"Because you're a woman?"

She sighed. "Yes. And because we have...history."

He squealed with delight. "Do tell."

She rolled her eyes. "It's not worth telling. We went to high school together, we...went out...once...it didn't work out."

"Oh, the drama! Is he *gorgeous?* You gotta love a man with a hard hat."

She massaged her temple. "I'm hanging up now."

"Of course, so you can go to Brass Balls. Sounds like a fun place. Want me to meet you there?"

"No, thanks," she said quickly. "But I appreciate you finding Langtry for me."

"Want me to send him a get-well bouquet?"

"That would be a nice gesture," she agreed.

"See you tomorrow," Price said. "And good luck with your old boyfriend."

Sam opened her mouth to correct him, but the dial tone sounded in her ear. She banged down the phone in frustration. This was shaping up to be a really lousy day.

And since she now had to find Teague and beg him to come back to the job site, it seemed likely to get worse.

CHAPTER FOUR

"NUMBER FIVE IN THE SIDE POCKET." Teague pulled back his right arm, then punched the cue stick forward to send the cue ball spinning into the five ball. The five ball went straight but hit the pocket hard and bounced back, to the delight of his playing partner, Griggs.

"Teague, man, I might actually beat you tonight. What's up?"

Teague walked over to where he'd set his beer, thoroughly pissed off that he couldn't get Samantha Stone out of his mind after their impromptu reunion today. "Nothing." He tilted up his longneck.

"It's that woman, isn't it?" Griggs pressed, then made his shot with little effort. "The one you dropped in the mud."

He and Griggs both still wore their work clothes—dirty jeans and shirts, mud-caked lace-up work boots that bore no resemblance to the trendy versions that so many people wore these days trying to look hip.

"No," Teague lied.

"Sure it is," Griggs said cheerfully, then sunk another

ball. "Why'd you do it? I've never seen you be disrespectful to a woman on the job."

Teague's mouth tightened. "I don't want to talk about it."

Griggs whistled low. "Man, she sure was a looker, wasn't she?"

He frowned. "I didn't notice."

"What, are you flippin' blind? The woman was stacked like a—"

"Just play, would you?" Teague took another swallow of beer, hoping it would banish the sour taste in his mouth. He had thought that humiliating Samantha Stone would give him a feeling of vindication for the way she'd treated him when they were younger, but it had left him feeling strangely unfulfilled. Dropping the woman in the mud when she damned well deserved it didn't begin to make up for the way she had cut him to the core.

"Speak of the devil," Griggs said with a laugh, leaning on his cue stick and nodding toward the door.

Teague turned his head and suddenly had trouble swallowing his mouthful of beer. Samantha Stone walked into the bar, overdressed and looking considerably cleaner than the last time he'd seen her. His heart beat a tattoo against his chest—he'd never seen her in here before. Chances were, her appearance wasn't a coincidence.

As he watched, she leaned toward the bar, giving the customers who were looking—and many were—a nice view of her curvy behind while she said something to the bartender. The bartender nodded, then pointed toward the pool tables and, more specifically, toward Teague.

"Oh, shit," he murmured.

"She's coming over here," Griggs said, then elbowed him hard. "She must be looking for you."

Teague frowned. "Shut up and take your turn."

But Griggs was right—Samantha had spotted him and had made a beeline in his direction.

He took another draw from his bottle, his mind racing with reasons why she'd hunted him down. To apologize for breaking his stupid heart all those years ago? To tell him that she was wrong for making him feel like he was important for a few illicit hours, only to slam him back into his place the next morning?

She walked up to him and seemed to hesitate, then her chest rose with an inhale. "Hi."

He studied her glittering blue eyes and acknowledged her with a nod.

She looked around awkwardly. "I, um, was told I could find you here."

He shrugged. "I'm here more often than not, I suppose."

She shifted in her designer shoes, looking hopelessly out of place in her elegantly draped slacks and filmy blouse next to the more casual clothing of everyone else in the bar. Her silky blond hair was pulled back in a low ponytail and he suddenly longed to see it swinging free.

"I was hoping we could talk," she said, her voice stronger.

He lifted his beer for a drink, buying time. "About what?"

She glanced at Griggs, who was studying them intently, then back. "Could we speak in private?"

Teague straightened, intrigued, then nodded and led her over to an empty table. A waitress came by and he ordered another beer, Samantha ordered a glass of wine.

When the waitress left, Samantha clasped her hands on the table in front of her. "I'm going to get straight to the point, Teague. I'd like for you to come back to the job site."

He raised his eyebrows, keenly disappointed that the reason she had sought him out had to do with business. "Why?"

She squirmed in her chair. "Because the site foreman, Mr. Langtry, is in the hospital and won't be able to fulfill his duties." She wet her lips. "He recommended that I ask you to take his place."

Teague was silent, distracted by the fullness of her mouth…. She had given him great pleasure with that mouth. And her left ring finger was empty—was she single? Had she ever been married? There had been women in his bed since Samantha, of course, some who had hinted at rings and weddings, but his heart had never been swayed.

"It's a tricky excavation," she continued, all business. "The site is narrow and steep, and I need someone who can implement my design for the retaining walls. According to Langtry, you're that person."

He studied her in silence until the waitress returned

with their drinks. So now she needed him. Satisfaction infused his chest. "Why do you think I'd be interested in taking the job?"

She sipped from her wineglass and shook her head. "I don't, especially after the note we...ended things on...today."

And thirteen years ago.

"But," she rushed on, "I hope that you'll consider it. It will be a chance to work with some innovative materials and techniques."

"*Your* innovative materials and techniques."

"Yes," she conceded. "And the site has to be ready in thirty days, rain or shine."

He pursed his mouth. "Why the tight time frame?"

She hesitated, taking another drink from her glass. "To be frank, the board of directors isn't convinced that the building I've proposed will work on the site, but they agreed to give me thirty days to prove my foundation design."

The wheels began to turn in his head. "So if you don't have the site excavated within thirty days, what happens?"

"I lose the project."

Even without the intensity in her eyes, he would have known how important the project was to her. During the night they'd spent together when they were teenagers, she had talked about little else than becoming a famous architect, erecting buildings that would impress her father. At the time, she had seemed desperate to get her old man's attention—he wondered if that was still the case.

"This is awkward," she said, splaying her hands, "but if you take the job, Teague, you and I will be working closely together. That doesn't bother me, but if you think it would bother you—"

"It wouldn't," he cut in. Was she so arrogant that she thought he was still hung up on her? Good grief, the woman was full of herself.

"Good," she said curtly. "So do you think it sounds like something you could do?"

"*Could* do?" he asked. "Sure."

She pushed the end of her ponytail behind her shoulder and Teague conceded that Griggs was right— she was a looker, all right. And the fact that he knew the passion that lay beneath her prim clothes and polished veneer had his sex pressing against his zipper.

"But *would* you, Teague? Are you willing to take the job?"

Willing to work side by side every day after being denied access to her when they were young? The thought of being close to her in a capacity where she would be seeking his advice left him almost breathless. It could be a way to explore his fantasies and prove to her what might have been if only she had given him a chance back when it would've mattered. In a way, he supposed he was as eager for her approval as she was for her father's approval.

She cleared her throat. "I'll pay you well."

At her words, an unpleasant knot lodged in his chest—she'd pay him well. That was all he was to her—

a laborer. A means to an end. But as he digested the finality of her words, an idea slid into his brain.

If ever there was a chance to put Samantha Stone in her place, to rob her of something meaningful, this was it. He could take the job and keep his crews busy while pacing everything so that they narrowly missed the deadline. The crew would then scatter and move on to more permanent job sites, where they'd rather be anyway. It was a win-win situation…for everyone but Samantha. She would get the comeuppance that she deserved, and he'd make sure that she knew he had planned it that way.

"I'll take the job," he agreed, hardening his jaw.

Her shoulders eased in relief and she smiled, an unexpected development that left him momentarily flustered as her face and eyes lit up. She thrust her hand forward, over the table, toward him. He stared at her manicured hand a few seconds before clasping it in his own hand, which was callused from wielding a shovel. Her skin was soft and cool, and her fingers squeezed his in a way that made his body clench with anticipation.

I'll pay you well. Her words resounded in his head and would, he decided, become his mantra to steel himself from falling for her again. This time he was in control. Teague squared his shoulders and gave her hand a firm squeeze in return. *Yes, Samantha, you will pay.*

CHAPTER FIVE

SAMANTHA WALKED TOWARD the job site, trying to calm
her jumpy nerves and smothering a yawn behind her
hand. She wished she could blame her previous night's
sleeplessness on her anxiety over the Carlyle project, but
she acknowledged that knowing she would see Teague
again today was what had her on edge.

She'd left the bar last night as soon as he'd agreed to
take the project, telling herself that she didn't want to
give him the chance to change his mind. In reality, she
had wanted to avoid the awkward "So what have you
been doing since high school?" talk. The less she knew
about Teague's personal life, the better. When he'd
clasped her hand in his to seal their agreement, she
couldn't shake the feeling that she'd just made a deal
with the devil, but she was willing to do whatever was
necessary to get the project off the ground. Working side
by side for thirty days with a man who so thoroughly
confounded her would be challenging, but she'd walk
on hot coals for thirty days if she had to.

It was midmorning, and the site already showed signs
of improvement and organization—knots of people

were working together in various areas of the narrow site, although she noted that the channel Teague had been digging yesterday had not been filled in as she'd instructed. Irritation blipped through her chest. Her eyes immediately went to Teague, tall and broad in the center of the site as he directed the driver of an earth mover where to dig. Her pulse quickened at the mere sight of him in Levi's and a pale-blue T-shirt, already sweat-stained beneath a climbing Texas sun. She tamped down her reaction—considering their history, it was natural that she experience some physical confusion where Teague was concerned.

Next to him, his chocolate Lab sat obediently, watching his master's every move. When Teague turned and caught Sam's eye, she felt the intensity of his gaze on her like an X-ray, as if he could see through her chino slacks and blue button-up shirt. She had dressed more appropriately today, with heavy-treaded shoes and her hair pulled back into a ponytail.

As she walked across the site, she was aware that a murmur followed her, with the workers remembering what she looked like doused in mud and probably theorizing what might have gone on between yesterday and this morning for Teague not only to be rehired, but now to be running the site.

"Good morning," she said as she walked up. The Lab walked over and sniffed her hand, then licked her cheerfully. She scratched his ears, smiling at his eager welcome.

"Mornin'," Teague said briefly. "Down, Dixon," he

said to the dog, then nodded toward the man standing next to him and to site plans unrolled on top of a pallet of cinder block. "Griggs and I were just going over some changes to the site plans."

Samantha's defenses rose like a wall. "Changes? There will be no changes—we don't have time."

Teague's head snapped back and his mouth tightened. "Your retaining walls are in the wrong place." He tapped the plans. "You have a wall here and here. But for this grade and for this type of soil, you need one here, here, and here."

She glanced at the map. "You mean where you were digging yesterday?"

He nodded.

Sam shook her head. "There isn't room with the utilities right of way."

"They would be smaller than the two larger ones you proposed, and more effective."

"But with my design for the retainer walls," Sam said, her ire rising, "two is all we need."

Teague pursed his mouth. "You asked me to run this site."

"That's right," Sam said, biting off the words. "But I expect you to follow *my* plans. Is that clear?" She'd spoken more vehemently than she'd meant to, but she couldn't have him questioning her design—and authority—on the first day. His eyes narrowed beneath the brim of his hard hat.

Next to them, the man that Teague had referred to as Griggs shifted uncomfortably.

"Clear as glass," Teague finally said, his words weighted.

"Okay," she murmured, trying not to flinch under his cool stare. "Perhaps now would be a good time to review the plans in more detail. When I explain the design, perhaps you'll see my point."

"Perhaps," he said, although he looked doubtful.

"Griggs," she said, looking at the other man, "would you see to it that the channel over there is filled in?"

Griggs hesitated, then looked at Teague.

Teague's mouth twitched. "You heard the boss lady."

Griggs nodded and walked away. Samantha looked at Teague. "I'm not the 'boss lady,' I'm the architect."

"Okay," Teague conceded in an infuriatingly aloof tone.

Samantha set her jaw. "About the retaining walls—"

"I have to go to city hall to file some paperwork," Teague cut in. "Why don't you ride along and tell me about these special walls of yours?" Instead of waiting for an answer, he whistled and strode toward his truck.

Sam frowned and followed him, wondering if the whistle was meant for her or the dog and hating that she had to trot to keep up with his long stride. When she reached the passenger-side door, she hesitated, nervous about being in such close confines with Teague. But since he didn't seem to be bothered by the idea, she yanked open the door and climbed inside.

From the driver's side, Dixon bounded up into the

space in the middle. Teague swung inside, set his hard hat on the dashboard and started the vehicle, seemingly oblivious to his passenger. Sam fastened her seatbelt and took advantage of the opportunity to study him, like she used to in biology class. His dark hair was shorter than he used to wear it and shot through with silver. His strong profile was much the same, except leaner, his cheekbones sharper, with a few lines around his eyes. She had the overwhelming urge to ask about his life, about what experiences had put those lines on his face, but resisted.

"That man Griggs," she said. "I saw him at the bar last night. Is he a friend of yours?"

"Yeah."

She bit her lip. "I didn't mean to embarrass you in front of him."

"You didn't."

"I just need for this job to be done on time and on budget."

"I said you didn't embarrass me." He glanced over at her as if he wished he hadn't asked her to ride along. "You were going to talk to me about these super-duper retaining walls?"

A flush climbed her neck, but she gathered her thoughts and began to explain the construction and ma-terials details and why the new design was perfect—and necessary—for the steep grade and soil type of the site. He asked a few questions, all of them on-point, and in the end she sat waiting with nervous apprehension and realized with a start that she wanted him to understand, to see the potential in her design.

After a few moments of silence, he pursed his mouth and nodded. "Interesting. Have you tried it before?"

She swallowed. "No."

"Well, for your sake, I hope it works."

She averted her gaze—it wasn't exactly the ringing endorsement she'd hoped for, but at least he seemed amenable to giving her idea a try…not that she'd given him a chance to refuse. Her cell phone rang and she removed it from her pocket.

"Hello?"

"Hi, sweetheart."

She winced. "Hi…Dad." She felt Teague's gaze cut to her.

"I called you yesterday."

How did he always manage to make her feel like a child again? "I'm sorry I didn't call you back. I just returned from New York and had to get started on the Carlyle project."

"I know. I'm coming to Dallas in a couple of weeks on business and I wanted to drop by to see how things are going."

She choked out a little laugh. "That's not necessary, Dad. But we can have dinner."

"And not see the site where my little girl is building her first landmark?"

Sam squirmed. "I'll call you later, Dad. I'm in the middle of something right now."

"Okay, sweetheart. I'll talk to you soon."

"Bye." Sam disconnected the call, feeling the curious vibe that emanated from Teague.

"I'll bet your old man is proud of you," he said finally.

She busied herself putting away her phone. "So, I heard rain is in the forecast for the day after tomorrow. Do you think the footers will be dug for the retaining walls by then?"

He looked over at her, his expression unreadable. "We'll try."

She had the sinking feeling that he'd just offered her an olive branch by asking her about her father, but she didn't want to discuss it. She looked out the window until the silence between them stretched taut. "How do you like Dallas?" she asked, to break the tension.

"Fine," he said, noncommittally.

One step forward, two steps back. "Have you lived here for a while?"

"Yeah."

So much for small talk. "Do you ever get back to Gypsum?"

"Not really."

"Me neither," she offered.

"Bad memories?" he asked mildly.

"Something like that," she admitted. Now that she was an architect, she understood how a house could affect a person's personality, could even contribute to a happy family life…or not. The palatial home she'd grown up in represented loneliness—she hated it, felt the despair squeezing her lungs every time she walked through the front door into the cavernous foyer. Only the guesthouse held good memories….

"Do you have family here?" she asked, trying to change the subject.

"Are you asking if I'm married?"

She squirmed. "I…was just making conversation."

"No—no wife, no kids. It's just me and Dixon."

At the sound of his name, the dog lifted his head and gave a low woof.

Sam patted his head, oddly pleased to know that Teague was still single. Odd because it wasn't as if they were going to pick up where they'd left off.

"How about you?" Teague asked, breaking into her troubling thoughts.

She blinked. "Me? I'm not married."

He gave a little laugh, a surprisingly pleasant noise. "You say that as if you have no intention of settling down."

Instead of answering, she continued to pat Dixon's head. The dog shifted and settled his head on her thigh.

"Careful," Teague warned. "He likes to be rubbed. You'll have to run him off to get rid of him."

His words vibrated in the air between them, and she had the strangest feeling he wasn't talking about the dog.

Teague wheeled the vehicle into the parking lot of city hall and cut the engine. "I'll be right back."

"I'll come with you," Sam said, climbing out. She didn't want to admit that she was unfamiliar with all the permits that needed to be applied for.

"Okay," Teague said, then lowered the windows enough to give Dixon plenty of air while they were gone.

She followed him into the building, surprised when he held open the doors for her. He seemed to know his way around, taking the stairs to an office on the second floor. The cute brunette standing behind the counter dimpled when he walked in.

"Hi, Teague. What can I do for you today?"

"Hi, Julie." He grinned and leaned into the counter, his body language easy and flirtatious. "I need to file paperwork for a new project site."

As he rattled off the form names, Sam wryly observed him interacting with the young woman as if they were old friends—no, lovers. An unpleasant feeling spread through her chest. Jealousy? Impossible, she decided. More like incredulity that the brooding, surly man could be so…likable.

Sam ignored the wary glances from Julie while Teague filled out miscellaneous forms. She recognized the look on the woman's face—she'd seen many girls in high school gaze at Teague Brownlee with similar adoration and longing. If Teague was still single, it was because he wanted to be.

She made a mental note of the forms he filled out, sober with the comprehension of just how much she was trusting him to manage and execute the job that could make or break her career. The thought had barely slipped through her head when he turned to lock gazes with her, his eyes dark and unfathomable…and oh, so sexy.

The realization hit her like a thunderbolt as incredulity swelled in her chest—she wanted him. Just yesterday she was talking with her friends about not getting involved with men who were beneath them in terms of respectability and earning power, yet here she was less than twenty-four hours later, lusting over...a *ditch-digger*.

Teague's lips parted and his expression grew wary. Sam averted her gaze and swallowed to regain her composure. Because the only thing more stupid than having a crush on Teague Brownlee was acting on it. She had fought too hard and now had too much at stake to let a man get the upper hand.

Especially this man.

CHAPTER SIX

"EVERYTHING LOOKS GOOD," Sam said to Teague, her chest expanding with satisfaction at the progress on the job site in only ten days. "Great job."

He nodded, which was, she'd learned over the past two weeks, the man's primary mode of communication. He didn't speak unless he needed to, and when he did he didn't waste words.

Dixon came bounding over to her and from her pocket she removed a chew toy that she'd bought for the dog on a whim. "Is it okay if I give this to him?" she asked Teague.

He shrugged. "Go ahead, but he's not much on toys."

She leaned over and offered the plaything to the dog. Dixon took it in his mouth without hesitation, then settled down at her feet to play with it.

Teague frowned and looked back to his clipboard.

Samantha glanced at Teague out of the corner of her eye, admitting that her respect for him had grown as she had observed him on the site. He didn't mind rolling up his sleeves (or, God help her, taking off his shirt) and pitching in to help when necessary, and it was clear that the men and women who worked for him held him in high regard.

Luckily, the weather had cooperated. In fact, it was the above-normal warm, dry temperatures that Samantha blamed on her constant state of restlessness and discomfort. Every day for over a week now, she'd awakened in the early hours of the morning, the sheets twisted around her overheated body. She'd attributed her insomnia to the pressure of the library site deadline, but standing next to Teague, she conceded that *he* dominated her thoughts— conscious *and* unconscious—more and more every day.

At the most inconvenient moments, snatches of the one night they'd spent together came back to her in vivid, sensory detail—the rough texture of his hands sliding over her skin, the naughty, adult words he murmured in her ear while he prepared her body to accept his, the erotic shock of seeing his work-tanned body melded with her pale one. At times the memories were so intense they made her gasp, at other times she had to cross her legs against the recollection of the pleasure he had shown her. And last night, in the shower, she had succumbed to the onslaught of erotic memories by gratifying herself with a soapy washcloth while fantasizing that Teague was with her, in his hard hat, no less, helping her to achieve release from his slow torment.

"Samantha?"

His voice yanked her back to the moment. "Yes?"

"Maybe you'd better find some shade," Teague said, peering at her. "You look sunburned."

She touched her flushed cheek and used a clipboard to fan herself. "I'm okay—it's just the heat."

"You know you don't have to come here every day. I'll let you know if there's a problem."

She bristled. "I have a lot riding on this project—I prefer to keep an eye on it myself." *And an eye on Teague,* her mind whispered, for reasons that had nothing to do with the job.

"Suit yourself," he said, then strode away. "Come on, Dixon."

The dog looked at her and whined but picked up his chew toy and loped after his master.

She cursed inwardly, regretting that she couldn't seem to be civil to Teague when in truth she was immensely grateful for his expertise on the job. She knew she wasn't a particularly easy person to work with—a woman had to be a little bitchy to make it in a man's world—but Teague left her confused and confounded. They could be having an innocent conversation and then *wham!*, suddenly everything that came out of his mouth seemed sexually charged. At times she couldn't tell if he was flirting with her or if her hormones were making her misinterpret entire conversations. As a result, their interaction was a confusing collage of short sentences, ambiguous innuendo and defensive body language.

It was, she acknowledged, a good thing that Teague was working for her. There was no way she'd jeopardize the project by becoming involved with him.

And then there was the fact that the man was a natural

leader yet seemed perfectly content to dig ditches. And what was it that Gerald Langtry had said? That Teague worked only when he wanted to. No matter how hot they would be between the sheets (and history told her that they could start a five-alarm fire), his intellectual malaise would eventually wear on her, she knew.

Which was exactly what she and Abby and Carley had discussed—looking past sexual chemistry to the traits of true long-term compatibility.

She watched Teague lift the tail of his T-shirt to wipe his face, her gaze riveted to the gleaming planes of his flat stomach. She moistened her lips and realized if she didn't get control of her wayward fantasies, she was going to go completely mad. She turned and tromped back to the company car that she'd brought to the site, determined to drive the image of a naked, sexual Teague Brownlee out of her mind. In twenty days, they would be finished with the job, and with each other.

TEAGUE TURNED TO WATCH Samantha walk away, his gut clenching at the sight of her swinging rear, from her tight ass to the tempting swish of her blond ponytail. His body hardened just watching her move—it was getting harder to work with her and not act on his attraction. And he had the feeling that she wasn't oblivious to the sexual sparks that flew between them even when they were discussing the most mundane of topics. Suddenly the routine subjects of contouring the land, tunneling channels and joining building materials made his cock throb. When the urge to touch her overwhelmed him, he picked up a shovel and joined his crew in an attempt to work his body to distraction.

He pulled his hand down his face to rein in his libido. As much as he wanted to bed her, he had to keep the end goal in mind…. He'd have her, but all in good time. The fact that she found him desirable didn't mean anything. She had found him desirable before—and unsuitable. Unlovable. This time would be no different, he reminded himself.

Debutantes occasionally went slumming when the uptown boys couldn't hack it in the bedroom. It didn't mean anything, didn't change how Samantha regarded him.

Meanwhile, the job was two weeks in and moving at a carefully controlled pace to prevent them from meeting the deadline. It was a shame, too, because he truly believed that the haughty Samantha Stone was onto something with her funky retaining walls. Deep down, that made him feel better because he knew there would be other projects for her in the future.

She turned back and looked at him, her lifted chin filling him with fiery resolve.

Other projects, maybe, but not before he took her down a notch.

CHAPTER SEVEN

"AND I WANT a fifty percent raise."

"Okay." Sam blinked, then jerked her head up to look at her assistant. "Wait a minute—what did you say?"

Price sighed and adjusted his tiny glasses. "Just as I thought. You haven't heard a word I've said."

She rubbed her temples and sat back in her desk chair. "I'm sorry, Price. I'm just preoccupied."

Price made a clicking noise and set a stack of folders in her in-box. "I don't suppose it has anything to do with the yummy ex-boyfriend?"

She glared. "I don't know what you're talking about."

"Tall as a tree, shoulders like a linebacker, eyes the color of a perfectly cut Colombian emerald."

Sam frowned. "Not that this conversation has anything to do with Teague Brownlee, but how did you know that his eyes are green?"

"Because he's in the lobby waiting to see you."

She lurched forward in her chair. "Teague is here? Why didn't you tell me?"

Price scoffed. "I couldn't very well just usher him to your office. You're much too busy to be so accessible.

I told him you were on an international video confer-
ence, and that you'd be with him soon. By the way,
you're fluent in French."

She narrowed her eyes at him but couldn't be angry.
She gave in to the smile tugging at her mouth. "How
long has he been waiting?"

"Thirty minutes."

Sam arched an eyebrow. "I think that's long enough
to prove a point, don't you?"

He nodded and grinned, clasping his hands in barely
controlled excitement. "I'll go get him."

His behavior only scattered Sam's nerves further.
The first day in three weeks that she hadn't gone to the
site, and Teague shows up at her office? Something
must be wrong—why else wouldn't he just call?
Before she could form another troublesome thought,
he was standing in her doorway, dressed in dusty work
clothes, looking rugged and handsome, with Price a
half step behind, beaming. "Ms. Stone, don't forget
your three o'clock appointment with the Carlyle board
of directors."

He had already reminded her twice—as if he needed
to at all—but she recognized that he was trying to make
her look good in front of Teague. "Thank you, Price."
She stood and smiled at Teague. "This is a surprise. Is
everything okay?"

"Everything is on schedule," he said, but wariness
flashed in his eyes as he took in her posh office view.
"I just came by to get your signature on a couple of

forms." He held up a file folder and handed it to her. "More permits."

She took the file and gestured to her guest chairs. "Have a seat."

"I've been sitting," he said wryly. "If you don't mind, I'll stand." Then he walked around her office, glancing at books on her shelves, picking up the crystal miniatures of famous buildings that she collected and setting them back down. He looked like a kid who'd been allowed into a room where he wasn't supposed to touch anything, but couldn't resist.

His thick hair was squashed and imprinted with the ring of a hard hat. From beneath her lashes, she studied him, watching the way he moved, the intimate fit of his jeans, the way the soft cotton of his gray T-shirt clung to his arms. She tried to tamp down the shimmer of desire that rippled through her stomach, but her body would have none of it. Beneath her fitted navy suit, her breasts grew heavy and her thighs tingled in awareness. All this from looking at the man's back, she realized in dismay. When he turned around, she dropped her gaze to the papers she was supposed to be signing.

"Looks like you've done well for yourself, Samantha," he said, gesturing to her office, her view.

"Thank you," she said quietly.

"Is it everything you thought it would be?"

She looked up sharply—was he referring to the hopes and dreams she'd shared with him the night in the guesthouse? Her heartbeat picked up speed and heat flooded her face. "I guess so."

He looked at her as if he were disappointed in her, and her defenses rose like a tide. Who was he to be questioning her? "You don't like my office?"

He shrugged. "It doesn't matter whether I like it, does it?"

"No." She pushed to her feet and walked over to the artist's rendition of the Carlyle Library. "But I would like to know what you think about my building design."

He moved to stand next to her to study the watercolor. At nearly a head taller than her, even with her wearing heels, he emanated male heat like a kiln.

"This project is really important to you, isn't it?" he asked.

She nodded. "I expect the Carlyle Library to set the stage for my career."

"Do you?" he asked, his eyes dark and unreadable.

Sudden sexual energy crackled in the air between them, catching her off guard. Her breath caught in her chest as she tried to remember what they'd been talking about. A muscle worked in his jaw and she couldn't tear her gaze away. Whatever was happening here, he felt it, too.

When he clasped her arms and lowered his mouth to hers, it seemed perfectly natural to respond. She opened her mouth, welcoming the warm tip of his tongue as his lips claimed hers in a powerful, hungry kiss. Her body pulsed with surprise and awe that he could make her feel so many things with just one kiss—anticipation, exhilaration, lust, and—

Her office door burst open and she wrenched her mouth from Teague's, appalled at her behavior. Worse still, her father stood at the door, his expression thunderous.

"That boy Friday of yours wouldn't let me in—"

"I'm sorry, Samantha," Price said. "I—"

Both men looked from Samantha to Teague. Her father gaped and Price gave her the thumbs-up.

Samantha's stomach bottomed out with shame. She wiped her hand over her mouth to see how much of her lipstick had gone astray and cleared her throat. "It's all right, Price." She conjured up a smile. "Hi, Daddy. I'm a little busy right now."

"I can see that," her father said, his mouth flat with disapproval.

Her gaze flew to Teague, who had turned away and was already moving toward the desk. "If you'll just finish signing those forms, I'll get out of your way."

She moved awkwardly to the desk, scanned the remaining forms and signed where necessary.

The fact that Teague still hadn't made eye contact with her father was not lost on her. He was reluctant to meet her powerful father, someone Teague probably had heard stories about for most of his life, especially after being caught kissing his daughter. Her father had a way of intimidating people, she conceded, despite his five-foot, ten-inch stature.

Price mouthed "Sorry," before slipping away, his

eyes twinkling. Samantha felt sick to her stomach. What had she been thinking to let Teague kiss her like that?

Teague's body language was rigid, his eyes wary as he watched Packard Stone walk toward the picture of the library. Sam knew just how he felt.

"This close to the end of the job, I thought you'd be on the library site, Samantha, so I went there first," her father said, his tone sarcastic. "I forgot that architects spend all their time behind a desk."

Her heart blipped with added apprehension. "I needed to spend the day here, catching up on phone calls and e-mail," she stammered, feeling like a schoolgirl.

"Uh-huh," her father said, obviously unconvinced.

She gave herself a mental kick. It was her own guilty conscience that made her feel as if she had to explain herself to her father. She glanced up at Teague, whose expression was unreadable. If the kiss had affected him, he wasn't letting on.

"And how was the job site, Dad?" she asked, to smooth over the awkward moments while she finished signing the papers.

"I saw those crazy retaining wall footers," her father said, and she suddenly realized the purpose for his visit. "They're simply not going to work," he announced flatly.

Her father had never had a problem with belittling her in front of other people, but to be chastised in front of Teague made her feel undermined—and humiliated. Her cheeks flamed as she handed Teague the folder of signed forms. "Thank you," she murmured.

He didn't respond, just nodded curtly and headed for the door. She watched him leave and when the door closed behind him, she was dismayed to feel a little less...strong. The sensation perplexed her because she was pretty sure that Teague agreed with her father.

When the door closed behind him, she turned to her father and crossed her arms. "Daddy, you can't simply barge into my office whenever you please."

He jerked his thumb toward the door. "Who the hell was that guy you were kissing?"

She squirmed. "No one."

"He looked familiar—and he had papers for you to sign."

She sighed. "He's the foreman on the library job site."

He looked incredulous, then his mouth tightened. "Well, that's one way to get the job done in thirty days."

She pinched the bridge of her nose, wishing she could hit the rewind button on her life. "It's not like that, Dad. What you saw just happened, it was a mistake." She didn't want to admit that the man she'd been kissing was one of the Gypsum Brownlees and they were only picking up where they'd left off in her father's own guesthouse. She sighed. "Let's just forget it, okay?"

"Okay," he said in the tone that indicated he'd bring it up later at the worst time possible. Then he opened his arms. "How about a hug for your old man?"

She smiled and went into his arms, inhaling the minty scent of his antique aftershave and closed her eyes. Despite his flaws, she loved him.

He broke the hug first and stepped back. "Do you have time for lunch? Dinner's out because I need to go to Houston tonight for some shindig with the governor."

"Of course," she said, and claimed her purse, trying not to be disappointed that he'd made other plans for dinner. The governor, after all, was more important.

They made small talk on the short walk to a restaurant around the corner and even though she was waiting for the other shoe to drop, she gave her father credit for waiting until they'd ordered before bringing up the subject again. "Sam, you have to rethink those retaining walls before it's too late."

She set her jaw, angry that he would be so vocal about something that wasn't any of his business. "Daddy, I'm twenty-one days into a thirty-day project. I'm not going to argue with you about my design."

A challenging light came into his eyes. "If you were working for me, I'd have you change them."

Doubts plagued her. Everyone questioned her design even though she'd spent years perfecting the engineering of the custom-made sheets of synthetic reinforced material to be used in place of standard reinforced concrete. Weary of defending herself, especially to her father, she spoke through clenched teeth. "But I *don't* work for you, Daddy."

His mouth twitched in suppressed anger. She remembered all the times he'd offered her a job and she'd declined because she knew she'd always be working in the shadow of his accomplishments, both in her father's mind and in the minds of the army of people who worked for him.

"And the executive committee must have thought that my design was promising—" she said, her voice stronger "—or they wouldn't have given me this chance to prove myself." She swallowed. "Stay out of this, Dad. This is *my* project, *my* career."

Her father's face reddened slightly, then he tossed down his napkin and stood.

"You'd better hope this excavation comes together, Samantha, because if you fail, *I* might be the only person around who'll hire you."

Her heart twisted as she watched him stride out of the restaurant. Why couldn't he just be proud of her? Why did he always have to be right?

Her mind went to Teague, and she was flooded with relief and gratitude that he had come back into her life at this critical juncture. His lack of ambition might not make him a great catch, but it had put him in the right place at the right time to rescue her project.

She touched her mouth where his lips had seared hers during their moment of recklessness. In her chest, her business sense warred with her guilt. If the kiss he'd given her was any indication of how he felt about his boss, he wouldn't let her down.

And although she had no intention of falling for Teague Brownlee, she needed him on her side for a while.

Samantha wet her lips. His hot, illicit kisses would simply be a bonus.

TEAGUE DROVE BACK to the job site, his chest tight with irritation over Samantha's father barging into her office. He wasn't sure what annoyed him the most—the fact that Packard Stone had intruded on his daughter's professional space only to criticize her design or that the man had interrupted a very promising kiss.

A kiss that Samantha hadn't shied away from, and in those few seconds, he'd gotten a glimpse of the passion he remembered when she'd lain in his arms all those years ago.

A little smile played on his mouth. His plan was working. Soon he would have Samantha Stone right where he wanted her—naked and underneath him, crying out his name. He'd seduce her, then dump her like she'd dumped him.

Dump her *and* the Carlyle Library project. In his wildest dreams, he hadn't imagined being able to exact such perfect revenge. He could show the Stone family that they couldn't simply use people, then discard them when they were through and expect to get away with it.

He reached over to pat the head of Dixon, who seemed grateful for the unexpected attention. The dog, who wasn't easily won over, constantly played with the chew toy that Samantha had given him, carried it around like it was some kind of special gift.

"Don't get too attached to her," Teague warned his pet…. Or was he telling himself?

CHAPTER EIGHT

"So what's new?" Carley asked.

Samantha was glad to be on the phone—if they were face to face, her friend would be able to see that something was bothering her. "Not much." *I can't stop thinking about a ditch-digger.*

"How's the library project?"

"So far, so good," she said cheerfully. *Except for the fact that my foreman kisses me as though I was paying him for it.*

"Are you avoiding all those unsuitable guys we talked about?"

"I don't have time for *any* guy," Samantha said wryly and, she hoped, convincingly. Then she bit her lip. "Although there is this attorney in my building."

"Ooh, do tell."

"We've just had a couple of conversations in the hallway. And the last time he saw me, I was covered in mud from head to toe."

"How on earth did that happen?"

"I, uh, fell on the job site." *Into the arms of a man*

who's gotten under my skin like a drug. "How about you? Any promising prospects?"

Before Carley could answer, Samantha's doorbell rang.

"Hang on, Carley. Someone's at the door."

She walked to the door and looked through the peephole to see Stewart Estes's angular, boyish face smiling back at her.

"Who is it?" Carley asked.

"My neighbor," Samantha murmured in surprise. "The one I was telling you about."

"He's making his move," Carley said with a squeal. "Successful and suitable—see, Samantha, I told you that if we held out, we'd meet someone worth investing our time in. Set down the phone. I want to hear his voice."

"What?"

"Indulge me. I'm living vicariously through you."

Sam sighed. "Okay." She set down the phone and thought about Carley's words. Successful. *Suitable.* Stewart Estes would be a welcome distraction from the inappropriate feelings she had for Teague Brownlee.

Pleased, she swung open the door. Stewart stood there, dressed in dark slacks and a thin, dressy T-shirt that skimmed his lean shoulders and arms. His hair was shiny with gel, and his tiny glasses were Versace. His skin shone with the glow of a recent facial—these days men with money took good care of themselves.

"Stewart. Hi."

"Hi, Samantha." He smiled and held up an empty

measuring cup. "This might sound corny, but I was wondering if I could borrow some sugar."

A flimsy excuse, but flattering nonetheless. "Sure. Come on in."

He stepped inside and hummed in approval. "Nice place. I like your decorating style."

"Thank you."

He took in her casual black velour sweat suit and appreciation flared in his eyes. "And you look…different than the last time I saw you."

She flushed and gave a little laugh. "That was a bad day at the office."

His eyebrows rose. "Where do you work?"

She told him the name of the firm. "But the day you saw me, I had been on a job site and I'd…had an accident."

"Ah." He nodded, but his eyes looked wary. "Does that happen often?"

"No," she assured him, then they lapsed into a tense silence of smiling and shifting. She wracked her brain for something to say. Had it been so long since she'd talked to a man about something other than retaining walls and site specifications?

"Well, I'll get that sugar for you," she said cheerfully. "How much do you need?"

"Oh, about a half cup should be fine."

She dipped sugar from a stainless steel container. "What are you making?"

"Uh…cookies."

She smiled. "An attorney who bakes? I'm impressed."

He blushed and stabbed at his glasses.

The doorbell rang again, and Sam frowned. "Excuse me. I don't know who that could be."

She handed the measuring cup to Stewart and walked to the door, then looked through the peephole. When she saw Teague's bottle-green eyes looking back at her, her heart skipped a beat. She straightened and glanced at Stewart. This could be awkward.

Swallowing hard, she opened the door. Teague stood there in dusty jeans and mud-caked work boots, his T-shirt sweat-stained and torn, a blue bandana tied around his head. His yellow hard hat hung from a loop on his belt.

"Hi, there," he said, oblivious to the fact that he looked so devastatingly sexy.

"Teague," she managed to say. "What are you doing here?"

"Sorry to bother you," he said. "We hit a snag on the site, a shelf of limestone that we weren't expecting. I think I know a way around it, but I wanted to run it by you tonight so we could get on it first thing in the morning." He jerked his thumb toward the elevator. "The guy in the monkey suit in the lobby tried to call, but your line was busy, so he told me to come on up."

"Come in," she said, repressing the urge to tell him to take off his muddy work boots.

He stepped inside, having left a trail of mud, she noticed, cringing, from the elevator to her door. She closed the door and suddenly remembered Stewart, who was still standing in the door of her kitchen holding the measuring cup of sugar.

"You should have said you had company," Teague said, eyeing the slender, well-dressed man.

"Uh, Stewart is a neighbor," she said quickly, then gestured toward Teague. "And Teague is a…a…"

"Employee," Teague supplied, bouncing the rolled-up plans against his palm.

"I was just getting some sugar," Stewart said, holding up the cup.

Teague gave him a flat smile. "You can never have enough sugar."

Samantha glared at Teague, then remembered the phone. Good grief, Carley had probably heard every word. "Excuse me." She picked up the phone. "Are you still there?"

"Are you kidding me? You have two guys there, and you think I'm hanging up? Who's Teague? He sounds hot."

"I'll call you back."

"But—"

Samantha disconnected the call, then ushered Stewart to the door apologetically. "I'm sorry. This might take a while."

"No problem," he said, looking Teague up and down, then he leaned in. "Are you sure it's okay for me to leave? He looks…unsavory."

One glance at Teague's rolled eyes told her that he'd heard every word. "No, it's okay," she whispered.

"I'll call you," Stewart said.

"Yes, do," she said, then closed the door behind him.

"Boyfriend?" Teague asked mildly, his voice full of amusement.

"No," she said, irritated. Then she lifted her chin. "Not yet."

He smirked, then walked over to the kitchen bar, leaving a trail of mud on the white carpet. Oblivious to the havoc his boots were wreaking on her floor, he spread the blueprints on the stainless steel surface and set four of her collectible (and pricey) crystal miniatures on each corner to keep the sheets flat. "He looks like your type," he muttered.

She followed, frowning at his audacity. "What's that supposed to mean—my type?"

"You know. Pristine."

She blinked. "Pristine?"

"You like complete order in your life," he said, then gestured to the stark white decor. "You want everything clean and in its place. It makes you feel as if you're in control."

She crossed her arms. "What's wrong with wanting to be in control?"

"It's boring. And it's unrealistic. You'll live longer if you learn to appreciate spontaneity." He gave her a look that said he was remembering their kiss.

Flustered, she willed away the heat that climbed her face. "You had no right to kiss me today."

He laughed. "You weren't exactly fighting me off."

"You…took me by surprise," she said, toying with the zipper pull on her velour top.

"And that makes you crazy, doesn't it?" His eyes mocked her.

She hugged herself harder. "Teague, I can't…we can't become involved—we work together."

"No. I work *for* you," he corrected.

She shrugged. "Whatever. I have a lot at stake here. We both need to stay focused on the job." Samantha was glad that her voice sounded stronger than she felt. And it was doubly hard to concentrate considering the hard hat that hung from his belt—the one she'd fantasized about in the shower. Having him and his hard hat mere steps away from her shower was a strain on her willpower.

His mouth tightened as he turned back to the papers. "How did it go with your father today?"

She considered lying—her relationship with her father was no business of his, but it almost seemed more of an effort to make up something that sounded good. Besides, she felt a strange compulsion to share with Teague. No one else among her acquaintances had been privy to the rise of Packard Stone in Gypsum and could appreciate the power that he wielded over those close to him. In hindsight, that night in the guesthouse she might have shared with Teague too much about her conflicts with her father. "It didn't go well. My father still thinks I'm a little girl."

"Fathers are like that."

"I suppose."

"I'm sure it's extra hard because you're in the same industry."

She sighed. "I have two college degrees, yet my father will never concede that I might know something that he doesn't."

"I think it's nice that you have so much in common."

"Do you and your father have a lot in common?"

He shrugged. "I guess we do. We both work with our hands. We both like the same things." He grinned. "Blondes."

She blushed, glad for the break in the tension. "Your mother is a blonde?"

He nodded. "She still turns my Dad's head. They never had two extra nickels to rub together when all of us kids were in school, but they toughed it out."

Envy pulsed through her chest that he had parents who were so in love. "I think that's…nice. Do your brothers and sisters still live in Gypsum?"

"Some of them. Some have scattered. I have a bunch of nieces and nephews."

She smiled. "Sounds like fun during the holidays."

"You mean total chaos." He gave her a pointed look. "You would hate it."

She squirmed, feeling like an uptight, hard-hearted person. "Big families sound exotic to me—and complicated."

"That they are," he agreed. "Did your father ever remarry?"

She gave a little laugh. "No. I guess my mother was

the only woman who could put up with him." She glanced away, mortified at the tears that gathered in her eyes.

"Hey," he said softly, turning her toward him and studying her face. "I didn't mean to upset you."

Feeling foolish, she blinked away the moisture. "You didn't. I'm sorry, I must be more tired than I thought."

"You must miss your mother," he murmured, stroking her cheek.

Surprised by his tenderness, she nodded. "Every day." Then she straightened and wiped the corners of her eyes. "So…show me the changes on the plans."

Instead, he reached for her hand and slowly pulled her against him. "We were interrupted today."

"Rightly so," she said, hating how prim her voice sounded and how hard her heart pounded.

"I kind of got the feeling that you liked it," he said, a lazy smile crawling across his mouth.

Heat infused her body as she remembered the kiss. "Like I said, you caught me off guard."

"Would you prefer that a man tell you when he's going to kiss you?"

A hum of desire sang low in her stomach. She swallowed hard. "A gentleman would ask."

His eyes darkened with desire as his mouth closed in on hers. "In case you hadn't noticed, I'm no gentleman."

CHAPTER NINE

TEAGUE'S MOUTH DESCENDED on hers in a burning, bruising kiss that chased all rational thought from her brain. His breath stole hers and she thought her lungs would explode from the pressure…and the pleasure. Giving in to the hunger that his rough kiss evoked, she gasped for air and wound her arms around his neck, oblivious to anything except the electricity that his mouth and hands unleashed in her body. His lips tasted salty, he smelled of man and musk, and the earthy aromas only heightened her excitement. She inhaled his scent into her lungs, smoothed her hands over his back and underneath his shirt to feel his warm, firm flesh and the indentation of his spine.

"Why are we doing this?" she whispered.

"Because it feels so damn good," he said with a growl, then captured her mouth with his before she could give voice to the doubts that skittered on the periphery of her mind. Doubts that disappeared as soon as his tongue touched hers.

He walked her backward until the edge of the bar pressed into her hips. The sting of the pain only keened her senses further, making her all too aware of his bulging erection pressing against her stomach. The kiss grew more aggressive as he leaned his body into hers. Frustration flared in her belly—frustration over being so incredibly attracted to him in spite of every reason not to be. She bit his tongue, seeing if he would back down, but he gave as good as he got, capturing her lower lip between his teeth, then nipping at her neck as if he might devour her, his breath ragged against her skin.

He stepped back long enough to unhook his hard hat from his belt loop and set it on the counter. Samantha stared at the object of her fantasy, knowing that by stripping himself of the bulky piece of gear, he was stating his intention to get a *lot* closer to her.

She looked into his green eyes, glittering with anticipation and promise, and she was lost. He traced a finger up to the zipper pull of her jacket and unzipped it slowly, caressing each inch of exposed skin. A shudder started at the back of her neck and traveled over her shoulders. She wasn't wearing a bra and her nipples beaded as soon as air hit her skin. He parted the soft fabric with his hands, his breath catching in appreciation as he palmed her full breasts. When his fingers closed over her nipples, plucking and pulling, she writhed in the most exquisite agony. The man knew how to make her body sing.

With a guttural groan, he lifted her and set her on the counter, sending crystal figurines rolling and smashing to the floor behind the counter. The elevation was perfect for his sex to press into the juncture of her thighs, and the promise of what was to come sent a flood of moisture to her folds. He lowered his mouth to each nipple, abandoning the gentle licks when she whispered, "Harder." He teeth and tongue became more insistent as he took and gave pleasure more roughly, tweaking her nipples with his calloused fingers until she cried out with delight. With her knees she squeezed his waist, clawing at his shirt.

He shed the shirt and her eyes went immediately to the angry red scar on his shoulder. She touched the puckered skin. "What happened?"

"Motorcycle accident."

"Are you okay?" she asked, suddenly concerned, but not entirely surprised to learn that Teague was still living on the edge.

"Fine now," he murmured absently, then dragged her velour pants and black panties down her legs, exposing her most secret places hidden by a downy thatch of dark golden hair. He gazed at her hungrily as he undid the fly of his jeans. She slid her hand into the front of his boxers and closed her hand around his thick erection to the satisfying tune of his long groan. Teague was a big man and amply endowed. His size had scared her a little when they'd spent that first night together, but now she knew how incredibly good it would feel sliding inside her.

He pushed at the waistband of his jeans to free his cock completely, then withdrew his wallet, presumably looking for a condom. He ripped open the package, then rolled it on in record time. Samantha leaned her hands back on the counter, but when her hand touched his hard hat, a naughty idea sprang to her mind. She picked it up and grinned. "Will you put this on for me, too?"

His eyebrows went up. "A little role-playing, huh? Whatever turns you on," he said on a ragged exhale that revealed he was hanging on to his self-control by a thread.

He put on the yellow hard hat and she shivered with pleasure at the sight of him, one hundred percent male, his broad shoulders toned and tanned from hard work in the sun, dark hair scattered across his firm pecs, winding its way down over a flat narrow stomach to where his cock jutted out, hard for her.

Her sex felt heavy, pulsing in anticipation. "I want you inside of me," she whispered frantically.

He rubbed the tip of his sex against her slick folds, then he clasped her hips and with a guttural moan, filled her in one thrust. The sudden fullness sent waves of pleasure crashing through her body. She gasped from the sensory overload that seemed to steal her mobility. She just wanted to float, and feel and receive his body. He began to grind in and out of her in long, powerful thrusts. She cupped his tight behind, reveling in the movement of his hips as he contracted to plunge into her, deeper and deeper until he reached her inner limit. He locked gazes with her, and she was unprepared for the passion she saw there. Mesmerized, she couldn't look away, reveling in the play of emotions over his face. His jaw clenched with effort and restraint, his eyes hooded with pure pleasure.

The sensations were so overwhelming that she could barely speak, barely hold herself up as their bodies slammed together. They were perfectly attuned to each other, on the same sensual wavelength. They moved together, faster and faster, each stroke more fulfilling than the last, until her body trembled with the strain of wanting, longing, stretching, reaching. With one massive thrust, he sent her over the edge. She cried out as her body collapsed in a crash of bright lights and intense spasms. A thought registered distantly that this was how she remembered it—this was the physical experience that had eluded her since she and Teague had last been together.

Teague watched her come, gratified at the languid abandon in her beautiful face coupled with the way her body contracted around his, urging him home. To see his cock imbedded in her nest of golden curls sent him to the brink of explosion. Unable to restrain himself any longer, he thrust hard and came, crying out with a force that weakened his knees and made him feel as if Samantha was drawing more out of him than his life fluid. His muscles contracted involuntarily, sapping his strength. God, she took him to the highest sexual peak he'd ever experienced.

As their bodies recovered, he clung to her, leaning into the counter for support. When he looked into her glazed, satisfied eyes, warning flags raised in his mind. *Get out now.* But he resisted the urge, telling himself that the worst thing he could do for his plan was to have sex and run. Instead, he gave in to the impulse to kiss her, capturing her lush, full mouth for a sweet, languid exploration to punctuate their shared experience. He pulled away from her gently and helped her down from the counter.

She reached for her clothes, pushing her hair behind her ears, suddenly shy—not the same woman who had asked him to wear his hard hat during sex, he observed wryly. She glanced at the paperwork they'd crushed, wrinkled and torn. He was afraid that the situation would jar Samantha back into her rigid state of mind, remorseful and ashamed. To his relief, she laughed, a sound that did strange things to his heart. "I hope they're still readable."

He grinned. "We might need some tape." Then he winced at the pile of broken crystal, the remains of one of the miniatures that Samantha obviously collected. "I don't think that tape will fix this. Sorry."

"It's no big deal," she said, waving away his concern, but frowning with regret at the same time.

He could tell that she mourned the piece—the great architect Ludwig Mies van der Rohe's Barcelona Pavilion. He felt bad. But he told himself if she didn't make a big deal out of it, he shouldn't either. Why was it that he had to remind himself to be cool when he was around Samantha Stone?

"Just give me a minute to get this cleaned up," she said. "Then we can get down to work."

He gestured vaguely. "Mind if I take a quick shower first?"

He noticed the slight hesitation, although she recovered well enough. "Down the hall, turn right."

He followed her directions, taking note of her immaculate decor. Even though he'd given her a hard time about it, it was refreshing to be in a woman's home and not feel like he was in the Land of Precious, with silk flower arrangements and hundreds of throw pillows covering perfectly good furniture. He walked into the bathroom, admiring the stainless countertops and slate-tiled floor. The entire room was a shower, with drains placed strategically in the floor. In the corner were two waterfall fixtures. Nice.

Then Teague turned and caught a glimpse of his reflection—naked from the waist up, with his fly undone, his arms dark with the day's dust, wearing his hard hat, like a damned gigolo. One part of him had been pleased to discover that Samantha was still an adventurous lover despite her prim facade, but another part of him had been dismayed that she was getting off on the idea of some Joe from her job site coming over to service her.

But didn't that only confirm that she still considered him to be beneath her?

He yanked off the hard hat and set it on the counter, then undressed and draped his clothing on a stool. He frowned at the mud that fell from the tread of his boots, but he had a perverse urge to dirty her carpet.

He turned on the water and stepped beneath the twin streams, leaning his hands against the wall and dropping his head to let the water flow over the back of his neck.

His body still vibrated and his mind still reeled from having sex with Samantha. She knew how to rock his world, but he had to remind himself that seducing her was only a means to an end. In a few days, the pre-closing inspection would expose his plan and he would, at last, have his revenge. These…*feelings* he was beginning to have for her were rooted in lust and retribution, nothing more.

Teague gritted his teeth. The thing that scared him the most was that he already wanted her again. He could almost still feel her hands on him.

Then with a start he realized that her hands *were* on him. He turned to see that she'd joined him, her long-limbed body stunning in its natural state, her breasts full, her waist narrow, her hips flared. And her eyes smoldered with passion. His body hardened instantly. She stepped under the tumbling water, ran her hands down his chest, then fell to her knees.

As she took his rigid cock into her warm mouth, Teague leaned his head back and steadied himself against the walls of the shower. Things were going way better than he'd planned…way better…

CHAPTER TEN

"And I want a Porsche Boxster as a Christmas bonus."

"Okay." Sam blinked, then jerked her head up to look at her assistant. "What did you say?"

Price crossed his arms. "Should I be worried about you?"

She smiled, feeling a little giddy. "I'm just preoccupied. The inspector for the library site is supposed to call today to let me know where we stand for getting things done by Monday."

"What do you expect him to say?"

She smiled wider, her chest expanding. "I expect him to say that everything is on or ahead of schedule."

Her assistant grinned. "Great." Then he angled his head. "But are you sure that good mood doesn't have something to do with that kissable foreman of yours?"

Her cheeks burned, although she couldn't deny it. "Did you come in here for a reason, Price?"

"Carley is on the phone and she says if you don't pick up, she's on the next plane here."

Samantha sighed. "Okay, I'll take it."

She waited until he left before picking up the handset and pushing the blinking light. "Hi, Carley."

"Don't 'hi, Carley' me! What the heck happened the other night? I've left you like, a dozen messages. I was starting to worry that those two men had had their way with you, then stuffed you under the bed."

Sam laughed and began to twirl a hank of hair. "No."

"No, they didn't stuff you under the bed, or no they didn't have their way with you?"

Distracted by her own memories, Sam suddenly realized that she'd taken too long to respond.

"You're twirling your hair, aren't you?"

Samantha stopped midtwirl. "No."

"Yes, you are. You got laid."

Sam blushed. "Well…"

"The lawyer made his move! This is great news! Abby's going to *die* when she hears you've snagged an attorney!"

Sam's throat closed—she couldn't very well admit that she'd gotten down and dirty with a ditch-digger, not after she'd been the most vehement of the three that they find someone who was their equal on all levels. Teague was a perfect physical specimen who knew how to push her most sensual buttons, but a long-term relationship was out of the question. There was, for example, that little matter of him working only when he wanted to.

Multiple orgasms notwithstanding, his voluntary un-employment would wear thin after a while.

"Are you there?" Carley asked. "How was it? Give

me details, woman—remember, I'm living vicariously through you."

"It was…fabulous," Sam said, unable to suppress a bubble of laughter. "We did it twice before we even made it to the bed."

"Oh, my God. Is he hung?"

Sam grinned into the phone. "Like a masterpiece in the Louvre."

Carley squealed. "And be honest—do you really care about this guy?"

Sam sat back in her chair and resumed twirling her hair. "It sounds weird, but, yeah, I really do. I can't explain it, but he's just so…noble. I feel safe when I'm with him."

"Wow, that's awesome, especially for the short time you've known him. So how did you get rid of Teague?"

Sam stopped twirling. "Huh?"

"You know, the other guy who showed up, wanting you to look at some plans or something."

"Oh…that guy." Sam pinched the bridge of her nose, reminding herself that Carley thought she'd been talking about her neighbor. "He's the foreman on the library job site."

"Oh, well I guess you couldn't hook up with him even if he *was* available, seeing as how you work together. But who cares about a sweaty construction worker when you've got an attorney who makes love like a porn star?"

"My thoughts exactly," Sam murmured, feeling miserable.

"What's his name?"

"Who?"

"The horny attorney—who do you think?"

"Oh. Uh, Stewart."

"Well, I'm really happy for you, Sam. I hope that what you and Stewart have will blossom into true love."

Somehow Samantha doubted it, considering Stewart had been walking by her door when Teague had left last night and she'd been wearing a robe. It didn't take a genius to figure out that the plans Teague had been holding weren't the only thing that had been rolled. And the strange thing was, she hadn't cared.

Sam's lips parted in sudden realization—she was in love with Teague Brownlee.

"You were right, Sam," Carley said. "All you had to do was decide not to waste time on any more unsuitable guys, and next thing you know you're having a wild fling with a guy who's not only great in bed, but successful, too."

Sam massaged the sudden discomfort behind her breastbone. "Right," she said weakly. Good God, what had she done? Fallen for a man who could never make her happy.

Yet he did, she realized in a wondrous split second of revelation. There was no denying that she just wanted to be around Teague, that he dominated her thoughts day and night. And no matter what he'd chosen to do with his life, he was the only man she'd ever known who could make her body come alive, who could talk about her work and who made her feel confident.

"Sam?"

Besides, digging ditches was not only an honest way to make a living but was essential for a project like hers to be completed. How could she have been such a snob? She'd almost closed her heart to Teague because he didn't aspire to a flashy, high-stress corporate job…because he wasn't chasing the almighty dollar, because he chose to do what he enjoyed and to lead a simple life.

"Sam? Are you there?"

A rap sounded on her office door, then Price stuck his head inside. "The inspector is on the phone."

Samantha's heartbeat picked up. "Carley, I hate to run, but I have to take this call about the library job site pre-closing inspection. Wish me luck. This could make or break my career."

"You have it. A man in your bed and a feather in your cap—sounds like you're having a banner week, Sam. Let me know how it goes."

Samantha said goodbye and disconnected the call. Price held up crossed fingers and backed out, closing the door. Sam sent a quick prayer heavenward, then pressed the button for the call on hold. "This is Samantha Stone."

"Ms. Stone, this is Daniel Fenton with the city inspector's office."

"Yes, Mr. Fenton, I've been expecting your call."

"I'm afraid we've got some problems on the Carlyle Library site."

Her stomach plummeted. "Problems? What kind of problems?"

He started reciting items, including permits that hadn't been applied for and ending with the more serious allegation that foundations for neighboring buildings hadn't been reinforced properly to ensure they weren't compromised structurally from the amount of dirt being displaced for the library foundation. There were concerns about water runoff and even soil samples that indicated they might need to dig deeper to reach more bedrock. The longer the list grew, the lower Sam's heart sank. "Did you review these items with my foreman, Mr. Brownlee?"

"Sure. He didn't seem concerned."

She sighed in relief. "So there won't be a problem addressing all these items before Monday?"

The inspector's dry laugh sounded on the line. "Monday? No way. Maybe a *week* from Monday if you can get your permits expedited and if your foreman and crew break their backs between now and then."

She tamped down the alarm that threatened to choke her. "That's impossible, Mr. Fenton. You see, the excavation has to be completed and pass a final inspection before Monday at eight a.m."

He made a rueful noise. "I don't know what to tell you, ma'am, but even if by some miracle you got things ready for inspection, it would take another miracle to get a city inspector out on the weekend."

Her breathing became shallow—this wasn't happening. "I...I need to speak to my foreman. How can I reach you, Mr. Fenton?"

He gave her his cell phone number. When she disconnected the call, she took a few calming breaths, telling herself not to panic…yet. She picked up her briefcase and headed out the door. Ignoring Price's questions, she left the office and drove to the library job site. To her dismay, the workers—what few of them remained—seemed to be packing up their equipment. She spotted Griggs and hurried over. "What's going on here?"

Griggs didn't seem to want to make eye contact with her. "The crew's moving on to another job."

"But you can't," she said, gesturing wildly at the unfinished site. "You have to complete this excavation first."

"Just doing what we're told, ma'am."

Frustration and anger billowed in her chest. "Where's Teague?"

"He left."

"He *left?*"

Griggs removed a slip of paper from his shirt pocket. "He said to give you this."

She took it and Griggs walked away, gathering his tools.

Bewildered, Samantha read the address written on the paper. Why would Teague leave her an address in an upscale part of town?

When realization dawned, her shoulders fell. He'd obviously found a new place to work and was taking his crew with him. A sense of betrayal washed over her. How could he leave her high and dry like this? And a deeper hurt pierced her heart—she'd fallen in love with him when apparently all he wanted was a roll in the sack for old times' sake.

She walked back to her car, pushing aside her raging emotions for the moment—she had to try to salvage the library project and her job. She programmed in the address that Teague had left for her into her car's GPS system. When she was underway, she took a deep breath and dialed her father's number. Her throat convulsed to swallow the pride that stuck there, but under the circumstances it was a call that she felt she needed to make.

"Packard here," he barked into the phone.

"Hi, Daddy—did I call at a bad time?"

"No worse than any other," he said sourly. "Are you okay, Sam?"

"I've been better," she admitted. "I need a favor."

"What?"

She forced as much strength into her voice as she could muster. "I just learned that the Carlyle Library site isn't going to be ready by Monday. I was hoping you would be willing to call Russ O'Bryant and ask him if the committee would be willing to give me another week." She held her breath waiting for his response.

"Did your foreman-loverboy let you down?" Packard asked drily.

She closed her eyes briefly. "Please, Daddy, don't go there."

"Sweetheart," he said finally, "you said I should stay out of this. I'm afraid this time, you're on your own."

She blinked back the sudden tears, hating herself for

asking in the first place—he was right, after all. This was her project to win or to lose. While she'd spent all her time worrying about her retaining walls, she'd let other important details get away from her, and she had only herself to blame. "I understand, Daddy. I'm sorry that I put you in an awkward position. I'll call you soon."

Sam disconnected the call and inhaled deeply. The GPS system beeped loudly, telling her she'd missed a turn. She pounded her fist on the steering wheel and turned around, hurt and puzzled over why Teague would abandon her job site for another. She turned into a posh, new neighborhood of palatial homes that she recognized as having garnered several awards for the developer. Some of the homes were finished and landscaped, some in various stages of completion from foundation to being under roof. The GPS system led her deeper into the neighborhood to the more established—and more expensive—homes on sprawling, wooded acreage. She leaned forward to look out the car window at the looming estates. Teague must have gotten a remodeling job or maybe some landscaping work. He was also going to get a piece of her mind.

To go along with the piece of her heart that he'd stolen.

"You have reached your destination," the GPS system announced.

She looked up at the soaring cedar plank and glass modern home nestled into a wooded lot. As she pulled into the driveway, she distantly acknowledged that she liked the mid-twentieth-century design, craning to spot signs of workmen on the grounds. Seeing none, she climbed out of her car and started down the side of the house, thinking the work was being done in the rear of the house.

Her pulse raced as she thought of what she was going to say when she saw him. There had to be some kind of mistake—maybe he thought the inspection of the library site was over and everything was fine, or maybe he misunderstood how important it was that everything be finished by Monday—

"Are you looking for someone?"

She pivoted her head to see that a tall man had come out onto the porch of the home. For a split second, the sun glare hid his face, but then he took a step forward and she blinked to take in what she was seeing: Teague, dressed in black slacks, a cream-colored shirt and expensive-looking dress shoes, holding a glass of red wine. On his wrist was a Rolex watch. He looked as if he were fresh from the shower, his dark hair gleaming and damp around his neck, and everything about him screamed money.

She frowned and moved toward him, her mind clogged with confusion. "Teague? What's going on?"

He gave her a flat smile and gestured to everything within sight. "Welcome to my home, Samantha."

CHAPTER ELEVEN

SAMANTHA STARED AT TEAGUE against the backdrop of the multi-million-dollar estate and felt disoriented...deceived.

"What's the matter, Samantha?" Teague asked. "Cat got your tongue?"

"This is your house?" she murmured. "But I thought—"

"That I was just a ditch-digger?"

"I..." She felt as if she were floating, lost, that the ground had fallen out from under her. "What's going on? Wh-why were you on the job site that day?"

His eyes glittered dangerously. "Why don't you come in, and I'll explain."

Curiosity and longing drove her forward. Moving in a fog, she climbed the long, shallow steps leading to the front door. He gestured for her to precede him and she stepped inside the house onto what looked to be a Tibetan rug, immediately captivated by the breathtaking spaciousness, the soaring ceilings, the enormous skylights that spilled sunshine into the house, decorated in a minimalist, masculine style. And unless her eyes deceived her, that was a Robert Motherwell painting on the far wall.

Across the expansive entryway, Dixon came bounding up to her, his toenails clicking on the rustic white ash flooring, carrying the chew toy she'd given him. He dropped it on the rug at her feet proudly and nudged at her hand for attention. She patted his head tentatively, suddenly unsure of herself…unsure of everything. She straightened and met Teague's gaze, astonished all over again at how stunningly handsome he was in his sleek designer clothes…although, she acknowledged vaguely, not more so than in his dusty jeans and sweat-stained T-shirt.

"Okay," she said carefully, "so obviously you're not a laborer. Why *were* you on the library job site that day?"

He touched his shoulder. "I found it was a great way to rehabilitate my injury. And I like getting back on the work site once in a while—it keeps me grounded."

Feeling like an idiot, Samantha crossed her arms. "And why did you let me believe that you were a construction worker?"

He shrugged. "Because you wanted to."

"But you let me…hire you." She fought back tears. "You humiliated me."

He gave a dry laugh. "You treated me as if I was a second class citizen because I was using a shovel, and *I* humiliated *you?*"

She put her hand to her temple, trying to make sense of his ruse. "What *do* you do for a living?"

"Mostly real estate investments now, but I did my fair share of moving dirt while I built my business."

Teague only works when he wants to. Samantha shook her head, baffled at his deception. "Why didn't you just tell me the truth?"

His eyes narrowed and he set down his drink. He stood close to her, close enough to touch. "I started to, when you offered me the job that night at the bar. But when I hesitated, you said that you'd pay me well. I realized that to you I'd always be a hired hand."

She started to deny his accusation, but she realized that she hadn't asked Teague for any details about his life, where he lived, what he'd been doing over the years. She'd simply…assumed. "So why did you take the job?"

His smiled was smug. "Because I saw my chance to get even with you."

She squinted. "Get even? You mean you took this job and purposely botched it so I would miss the deadline? Lose the library project?" She stared, incredulous. "Why would you do something like that?"

A look of disgust came over his face. "Did you grind people under your heel so often that you don't remember?" He reached into his back pocket and removed his wallet. "Let me jog your memory. I was a clodhopper with a crush on the most spoiled little rich girl in school who wouldn't give me the time of day—until I crashed your party and you let me spend the night in your bed."

"And that was one of the most memorable nights of my life," she murmured.

"Really? Do you *remember* leaving this note when

you left?" He removed a folded scrap of paper from his wallet and handed it to her.

She took it with trembling hands and opened it to read her own handwriting. *Don't track dirt on my carpet when you leave.*

Her eyes filled with tears at the callous young woman she had been—too worried about getting into trouble and too eager to rid herself of his memory to consider how the note might have come across to Teague.

"You didn't have to remind me that I was dirt-poor trash," he bit out. "I knew that pretty well all on my own."

"I didn't know you'd take it that way," she said. "I didn't think that night had meant anything more to you than bragging rights to your buddies." She struggled to hold back her tears. "All of this—the job, the seduction—it's all been part of a master plan to...to put me in my place?"

A smug look settled on his face. "It worked, didn't it?"

Her cheeks felt wet, but she managed a smile. "Yes. It worked, Teague. You win. The joke's on me because not only have I lost the biggest project of my career, but I also fell in love with you."

Teague blinked. He'd expected Samantha's anger but not her tears. Oh, maybe the ranting tears of a spoiled woman but not the dribbling tears of someone who seemed...hurt. Then he reminded himself that hurt to Samantha Stone was just a temporary inconvenience... any hurt she might be feeling was simply a bruised ego, nothing compared to the bone-cutting hurt that she'd inflicted on him with her careless, cruel note. The kind of hurt that left a young man feeling as if he'd never be good enough, that made him work harder and longer to achieve the monetary success that would fulfill him, that would force other people to look up to him.

Cynicism curled his mouth. "How convenient of you to suddenly proclaim your feelings for me after you realize that I'm not just a lowly ditch-digger." He shook his head and emitted a harsh laugh. "No, I'm not going to fall for that again. As far as your precious library goes—there will be other projects. After all, you're not the kind of person who will settle for less in life than you deserve."

He walked past her and whistled for Dixon, who looked up at Samantha and whined.

"Dixon," Teague said more firmly, *"come."*

The dog looked at her with mournful eyes, then picked up the toy and followed Teague.

Teague glanced down at her shoes, soiled, presumably from the job site. "Don't track dirt on my carpet when you leave."

CHAPTER TWELVE

SAMANTHA STOOD ROOTED to the floor watching Teague and Dixon walk away, waves of painful emotion breaking over her—degradation, humiliation, betrayal, anguish, heartbreak. She had thought when her mother died that that was as alone as she would ever feel. But her mother hadn't left willingly, hadn't dangled her love like a carrot, snatching it away when Samantha reached for it. *This,* Samantha realized, watching Teague walk away, *this is loneliness.*

Swallowing against the ache that lodged in her throat, she backed out of the door, kneeling to brush away the dirt her shoes had left on the expensive rug before pulling the door closed.

She made it to her car by putting one foot in front of the other, slid behind the wheel and hit the return-trip button on the GPS system so she wouldn't have to think about the traffic or the turns to get back home. She was still numb when she walked onto the elevator in her building.

"Hi."

She turned her head to see Stewart Estes standing there in his pristine suit, his eyes slightly guarded.

"Hi, Stewart," she said, conjuring up a small smile before glancing away.

"Are you okay?" he asked. "You look…upset."

"Bad day at work," she said. "I'm fine, but thank you for asking."

He nodded stiffly and turned back to the control panel but waited politely for her to precede him off the elevator when it stopped on their floor. She walked to her door, feeling like such a fool—with a perfectly nice guy borrowing sugar from her, how could she have fallen in love with Teague Brownlee?

Because he made her feel alive, and he made her feel adventurous, and he made her feel like there was more to the world than what she had created in her own little corner. He drew her out of herself…but apparently not enough to truly see him.

Teague was right—she hadn't treated him fairly when they were younger, and when their paths had crossed again she had jumped to false conclusions about him based on his appearance and her expectations of him. Then she'd thrown money at him and taken for granted that he would handle the messy details of the job site, that he would cover her, not just because he was an employee but because of the superior/subordinate relationship they'd always had.

Her arrogance had not only cost her the love of her life but the job of her career.

And she couldn't blame her father for the snob she'd grown into—how many times had he said that no matter how much he trusted his employees, the buck stopped with him—he checked every detail of an important job himself.

She closed the door behind her and straightened, shaking off her personal despair over Teague—she had the rest of her life to brood about what might have been, but she had only two more days to come up with a plan to salvage the library project. She bypassed the counter where just days before Teague had spread plans for them to study and had instead wound up making love—correction...*having sex.*

Pushing the erotic images out of her mind, she headed for the drafting table in her den. Without a crew, she couldn't do anything to the site before the Monday morning meeting, but she could prepare a passionate presentation for the board of directors, accept blame for the job delay and ask for more time. In return she'd offer to forego the design details of the library that would have been her signature in order to trim the budget.

It would be a humbling experience but necessary.

She went into the bathroom to change clothes and spotted Teague's yellow hard hat. Her face burned when she remembered asking him to wear it while they had sex. He must have felt belittled, used...manipulated. She didn't blame him for hating her...she hated herself for behaving like a debutante sleeping with the hired help.

Feeling sadly wiser, Samantha changed clothes,

brewed a pot of coffee, spread the current plans for the library on the drafting table and settled in for a marathon work session.

DIXON WHINED and dropped the chew toy that Samantha had given him at Teague's feet in front of the leather club chair where he sat in his big, empty office.

Teague frowned. "Get over it, buddy." Then he took another drink of bourbon from his glass. Two rounds of the stuff hadn't erased from his mind the stricken look on Samantha's face when he'd told her that he'd been playing her all along. Instead of the sense of vindication he'd expected to feel, a stone of guilt had dropped to the bottom of his stomach and had grown heavier since she'd left—after brushing away the dirt on his stupid rug like he'd asked her to do.

He put the cold glass against his temple, hoping the chill would jar him out of his funk and remind him that Samantha deserved everything that she'd gotten. Dixon put his warm head on Teague's knee and looked up at him with the most sorrowful eyes imaginable.

Teague sighed and put his hand on his pet's head. "I know how you feel." He set down the glass of bourbon and pulled his cell phone out of his pocket. He flipped it open and punched in a number, relieved when it was answered on the first ring.

"Griggs, it's Teague. I need your help."

CHAPTER THIRTEEN

SAMANTHA PULLED UP to the job site Monday morning wearing sunglasses to hide her lack of sleep and a Dolce & Gabbana pant suit to boost her confidence. Even though she was early, to her dismay, several cars were already in the parking lot. The last thing she wanted was to be perceived as not caring about the deadline, especially since she hadn't met it. She grabbed her briefcase and hurried toward the site, her stomach in knots.

Russ O'Bryant and four other members of the board of directors stood peering out over the site. She hoped that the fact that the site had come so far would help them to visualize the building she had proposed.

"Good morning, Mr. O'Bryant," she said.

His jowly face creased in a wry smile. "Good morning, Ms. Stone. Cutting it a little close, wouldn't you say?"

She looked to where he indicated and frowned at the hordes of workers streaming away from the site toward their vehicles parked all around the perimeter. Two men in particular stood out in the center of the job site—one of them, she realized with a start, was Teague, in his work clothes, complete with hard hat and with Dixon at his side.

Samantha inhaled, her heart clicking overtime. What was he doing here?

As she watched, Teague accepted what looked like a folder of some kind and shook the other man's hand, who then walked away. Teague turned and strode toward the group, his gaze tracking hers. Dixon spotted her and ran ahead, bounding up to lick her hand.

She smiled and petted the dog but was dismayed to realize that despite everything that had happened, her body still reacted as Teague approached, her senses reeling. It was going to take a long time to get over him.

"Good morning, Ms. Stone," he said formally, removing his hard hat. His hair was flattened, his face, neck and arms almost black with grime, his clothes sweat-stained. He had never looked more handsome to her.

"Good morning," she managed, confused.

"Here are the inspection reports," he said, thrusting the folder into her hand. "I think you'll find that everything is in order. The site is ready, with all paperwork filed and approved." He swept his glance over the directors to include them. "You'll be happy to know that the site passed the engineering inspection with flying colors. And the engineer was especially complimentary of the design of your retaining walls, Ms. Stone. I told him I expected the patent would be filed shortly."

Sam was speechless. She felt the file folder in her hand, but she couldn't believe what she was seeing…and hearing. "I…I…" She glanced at the directors. "Would you excuse us for a moment?"

Sam waited until she and Teague were out of earshot before she turned to him. "Is this another joke? Another setup?"

"No," he said flatly, his eyes serious.

She shook her head. "I don't understand."

"I was wrong," he said simply. "I shouldn't have done what I did to you, Sam. After you left my house, I made a few phone calls, got some crews and equipment back out here, and called in a few favors at city hall." A rueful smile lifted his mouth. "Besides, I wasn't about to give your father a chance to gloat. And don't worry about the added cost—it's on me."

The expense, she was sure, was little more than a rounding error on his personal balance sheet. But she knew that he had performed miracles to get the job site overhauled in little more than forty-eight hours, not to mention getting the inspector out before dawn.

"I don't know how to thank you," she murmured, feeling completely humbled.

"You don't have to thank me," he said, then settled his hard hat back on his head. "I was just doing my job."

As he started to walk away, she said, "Teague."

He turned back.

"I'm sorry…for everything. I hope you can forgive me."

His green gaze seemed to laser into her soul. "Same here."

He whistled for Dixon, then walked to his truck parked alongside the road, climbed in and drove away.

"Goodbye," Sam whispered, her heart drowning in her chest. The Carlyle Library project was hers, but the victory felt bittersweet. She winced inwardly at the pact she had made with Abby and Carley in her arrogance—she'd been so determined not to fall in love with a man she considered to be beneath her, and now she was the one with the broken heart.

CHAPTER FOURTEEN

"CONGRATULATIONS!" Carley's voice rang out over the phone. "I'll bet your dad is so proud."

"Yeah," Samantha said, fingering the silky petal of a white lily in the huge flower arrangement her father had sent to her office with a card that read "I knew you could do it—you're a Stone!"

And, true to form, Packard had also left a voice message on her phone, telling her to let him know when she was ready to move forward with the patent on her retaining wall system. She smiled and shook her head, but she couldn't hold a grudge against him—everyone was wrong sometimes. Only sometimes it cost a person more than she could have imagined.

Teague's face popped into her mind as it had so often in the past week since he'd walked off the job site and driven away. It had been the longest week of her life.

"So, are things still hot and heavy with the attorney?" Carley asked.

Samantha pressed her lips together, thinking that the only good thing about Teague dumping her was that the girls would never know that she'd reneged on their pact. "Uh, well, things have cooled down a bit."

"Oh, no! What happened?"

A rap sounded on her door, and Price stuck his head in, his eyes as round as coasters. "You have a visitor," he whispered in a rush. "It's your *foreman,* but he looks...*different.*"

Her vital signs went haywire. "Carley, I have to go."

"Wait—tell me what happened!"

She hung up the phone while her friend was still protesting.

Teague walked in, breathtaking in a dark olive suit that complemented his dark skin and deep green eyes. He carried a small box. Price pointed at Teague's jacket and mouthed, "Armani," then backed out and closed the door.

Despite his impeccable grooming, Teague looked uncomfortable. "Did I come at a bad time?"

She stood but averted her gaze, afraid that she would telegraph the feelings she still had for him. "No, this is fine. Um, won't you sit down?"

"Thanks, but I only came by to give you this." He extended the box stiffly.

Sam frowned but took it and opened it, then smiled in surprise to see a replica of the crystal miniature that had been shattered when they'd knocked it off the counter in her condo. "The Barcelona Pavilion. You didn't have to replace it, but...thank you." Her cheeks flamed when she remembered what they had been doing at the time.

"Actually," Teague said, "I wanted to thank *you*, Samantha."

"F-for what?"

"For showing me what a hypocrite I was," he said quietly. "I did exactly what I accused you of—I misjudged you because of your circumstances and your appearance. I assumed you were still daddy's little girl, getting ahead on your father's reputation and money." He shifted foot to foot, then made direct eye contact. "You're a talented architect, and your retaining wall design is brilliant. You have my utmost respect, and I know that the Carlyle Library will be the first of many successes."

She blinked in astonishment at his speech, tamping down the emotion that crowded her chest. "That means a lot to me, Teague."

"I'll be going now," he said, moving toward the door.

Her heart sank, but she nodded, smoothing her hand over the tiny details of Ludwig Mies van der Rohe's Barcelona Pavilion. She had always wanted to see it in person, but now it would only remind her of Teague.

"Samantha?"

She looked up to see him standing with his hand on the doorknob.

"When you came to my house, you said you loved me." His Adam's apple bobbed. "Did you mean it?"

She set down the miniature and nodded, no longer caring if she looked foolish. If he needed to hear how completely he'd conned her, it was a small price to pay for him delivering the site excavation on time. "I didn't tell you sooner because…I didn't want it to affect our working relationship." A dry laugh escaped her. "Considering everything that's happened, that's pretty laughable, huh?"

A muscle worked in his jaw. "No." He walked back to her desk, his expression sending her heart pounding against her breastbone. "The thing is…I mean, what I should have told you sooner…and I don't expect you to believe me, but…"

She squinted. "But?"

He looked like a tortured man as he struggled for words, then it seemed as if something inside of him broke loose as his gaze met hers. "I love you, too, Sam. I always have, since we were kids." He exhaled noisily. "But after what I did to you," he said, his voice shaking, "I'd understand if you wanted me to just…go away."

Sam went very still, absorbing the enormity of his words and how they might affect her life, if she so chose. Two heartbeats passed, three, four… "Yes, Teague—go away."

His eyes clouded, but he nodded and started to turn.

"With me."

He turned back, his expression questioning.

"Go away with me—" she said, walking around the desk "—to Barcelona…to Sydney…to the North Pole." She smiled through her tear-filled eyes and looped her arms around his neck and whispered, "To bed."

He groaned as he wrapped her in his arms. "Woman, you're going to be the death of me."

Then he lowered his mouth to hers in a hungry, full-body kiss that promised a future of spirited adventures and torrid lovemaking. With his arms around her, Samantha realized that the last time she'd felt so wildly optimistic about the future, she'd been lying in Teague's arms when they were teenagers. So much had changed, only to bring them full circle, that it was almost too much to comprehend. She closed her eyes and breathed this man's essence into her lungs, trying to get used to this feeling…happiness.

Then she stepped back and smoothed a hand down the lapel of his fine jacket. "You know, I rather like this suave, sophisticated side of you."

He nuzzled her neck. "You do, huh?"

"Uh-huh. But I wouldn't mind if you wanted to wear your hard hat once in a while…privately."

He laughed in her ear. "I think that can be arranged."

Teague picked her up and swung her around, and Sam's heart stretched with joy. She couldn't ever remember being so happy, and, in fact, she had only one problem—explaining to her friends Abby and Carley that she'd literally fallen head over heels in love with the very type of man that she swore she would never date!

But that could wait until later. *Much* later.

THE TOTAL PACKAGE

Jennifer LaBrecque

CHAPTER ONE

"I WANT A WOMAN."

Abby Vandiver placed her pen on the desk, sat up straighter in her hi-back leather chair and really looked at Deke Foster, chief computer guru for Mansell and Cowart Limited, MCL for short. She'd waved him into her office when he knocked but she'd been too focused on wrapping up her recommendations on her current project to take much notice of him. And obviously she'd misheard what he'd said. Because she could've sworn he'd just declared he wanted a woman…and, well, that would be weird in the extreme. Not weird that he'd want a woman, but that'd he'd tell her.

"I'm sorry, I needed to finish up some notes," she said, shifting mental gears and offering him a smile. "Is there a problem with one of the software update releases?"

Deke pushed his glasses back onto the bridge of his nose. "Uh, no. No problem with the software update." He shoved once again at his glasses, even though they hadn't slipped in the last two seconds. "I'm here because I want a woman."

She *had* heard him correctly the first time. Deke, in a professional capacity, had always struck her as a geek, but a nice geek. Never weird. Until now.

"And you're sharing this with me because…?"

"Because I need you."

Abby steepled her fingers, torn between flattery and apprehension. Why should this surprise her? Hadn't she just had this very discussion with Samantha and Carley? She was a loser magnet. And hadn't they just toasted to no freaks, geeks, and generally unsuitable guys that topped the No Date List? "That's very kind, but I'm not the woman for you, Deke." In the year that he'd headed up MCL's IT division, they'd barely exchanged a dozen words outside of discussing mutual projects.

He looked almost resigned, as if he'd expected her rejection. "I didn't mean I want you personally. I just need your help. Your expertise."

Okay, then. This was getting curiouser and curiouser. His personal dismissal of her should have stung—perhaps it did a bit, but she was far more interested in why the company's reclusive computer whiz had sought her out. "My expertise in what? For what?"

Deke's puppy-dog brown eyes stared back at her from behind thick glass lens's. "You're the marketing wunderkind. You can take anything, change the packaging, remarket it and it becomes an instant success. You're a marketing/packaging genius."

He was right. She was. She'd really found her niche

at MCL, one of the country's foremost consulting firms specializing in consumer products marketing. Everyone had a talent and that just happened to be hers. "Okay?"

"I want a woman. Make me over. Rework my packaging." She bit back a smirk as the sexual connotation of his *package* came to mind. He was laying the facts out sequentially as a person versed in logic would do while she made mental sexually inappropriate jokes. Maybe working through lunch today wasn't such a good idea. It'd left her a little light-headed. "Please, save me from geek-dom," he implored. His logic gave way to an intensely personal appeal.

He recognized his geekiness. So, he got points for self-realization. He "wanted a woman." She shook her head. She wasn't in the business of female procurement. She was a business professional, not a madam. And she certainly wouldn't fix him up with any of her girlfriends. Even if they hadn't sworn off geeks, freaks, ditch-diggers and used car salesmen, Samantha would chew him up and spit him out. Carley wouldn't want to hurt his feelings, but she wouldn't be interested. "Deke, if you're looking to hook up for sex, find someone else to help you."

"I don't want sex. I mean I do. Of course, I do." A dull red rode up the column of his neck. "What I mean is, I want a wife."

Oh.

Marriage. Supposed permanence. Commitment. Female procurement seemed more ethical. And it'd be so much easier for him down the road. Carley had deemed Abby cynical. Practical was more accurate.

"Wouldn't you rather just have sex?" She'd feel better about *that* than leading him to the less-than-rosy path of matrimony. It smelled sweet, but, as she well knew, it was also thorn-ridden.

"I want a wife." He fiddled with his plastic pocket protector but stood firm.

"Why?" He was in his early thirties. He should know better by now.

"I want someone to come home to every night. Someone to share things with." She knew a flash of recognition. Once upon a time, she'd craved the same thing, but then she'd found the price attached was far too high. Now she was perfectly content on her own. Okay, so perhaps not *perfectly* content, but content enough.

Not that she wouldn't enjoy dating, but she wanted nothing to do with marriage. Deke, as did most people thinking about tying the knot, had no idea what he was actually asking for—the heartache, the betrayal, the emotional blackmail.

"You don't need me. Go to the pound. Get a dog." Adopting Minerva, a black and white Chihuahua who bore a striking resemblance to a fruit bat, had seen Abby through her divorce and some tough times. Back then, Minerva had given a damn when she came home at night and six years later, the little dog still cared when Abby showed up. And she'd like to think it was more than just because Abby fed her. Trite as it sounded, Mini offered unconditional love—although treats did engender additional canine devotion. And she'd proven far more loyal and far less egotistical than Abby's ex-husband.

"I have a dog. I want to start a family."

Forget the dog angle. They were back to square one. She supposed he did need a woman for that. Abby rolled her chair back and stood.

"You're leaving?" Deke asked on a panicked note.

"No. I'm evaluating you." She rounded the desk, the thick carpet absorbing her footsteps. "Would you stand up and step away from the chair?"

He rose and shifted away from the leather-bound armchair. Deke stood in the middle of her neutral carpet, his arms crossed self-consciously.

She circled him, studying him the same way she might dissect a product for re-packaging.

She was five-seven in her two-inch heels and he still had several inches on her so she'd estimate he stood around six feet. Shaggy brown hair fell past his collar but didn't hit his shoulders. But it wasn't the sexy, longish look that was in vogue. At least it was clean. Still, a scruffy beard all but obscured his face.

She paused. Black rimmed glasses framed serious brown eyes that were actually very nice with their fringe of thick dark lashes. She'd never noticed his eyes hidden behind those glasses before. A small shiver chased down her spine. His eyes were really quite…well, sexy. She pulled herself together and moved on.

From the head down it was anyone's guess. A plaid

tie waged war with a striped shirt. She bit back a grimace. Dreadful. Just dreadful.

"Are you colorblind?" she said. Many men were and it would explain a lot.

"No." He glanced down at his shirt and plucked at his tie with a puzzled expression. "They both have green in them."

She nodded. "Uh-huh." Okay, so he wasn't colorblind but he'd obviously missed the class on successfully pairing companion prints.

His navy Chinos were inoffensive but accentuated his startling white athletic shoes. And his clothes were all too big.

"Okay. Thanks. You can sit back down, now."

She returned to her side of the desk and sank into her chair.

Deke Foster epitomized every geek cliche. He could've been the poster boy for geekdom. A faint tingle raised the small hairs on the nape of her neck. There it was—that frisson of excitement she always felt before taking on an exceptionally challenging project. This might well top the list. She'd be crazy to do this. She was already busy and…well, Deke was a mess. Except for those eyes, which were all the more disconcerting because they were so unexpected.

"Why should I do this?" Abby broke the silence with her challenge.

"It's obvious I need help. And you're the best.

Someone as successful as you isn't in it for the money. You like the challenge."

Abby inclined her head in acknowledgment but didn't speak. He was very perceptive.

He folded his hands in his lap. "If you won't help me, I'll try Lyle Turner next," he continued.

Abby bristled at the mention of her arch competitor. And ex-husband. Lyle was a class A-jerk with an incredible ego, although he hadn't always come across that way. Obviously she wouldn't have married a known jackass.

Nope, once upon a time, she and Lyle shared many common interests—the same field of work, ambition, talent. Things were fine for the first few years. He loved her success and her income until both exceeded his. It was at that point that Lyle developed a driving need for children. They'd start a family and she could stay at home, working part-time or quitting altogether. Lyle had delivered an ultimatum—her career or him.

Abby opted for door number one, her career. She'd traded Lyle for Minerva and her only regret about the whole thing was her naïveté regarding marriage. Even now, she still winced at her foolishness. She'd lived the train wreck of her own parents' marriage so why had she expected her own to be any different? Maybe she hadn't. Maybe she'd just been waiting for the other shoe to drop from the moment she'd said "I do."

Regardless, it had hurt. But none of that mattered now. Within months of their divorce, Lyle had remarried and a year later his new wife presented him with a bundle of joy. Now Lyle boasted two kids, a wife, and a home in the suburbs. And he was still pissed that Abby remained one step ahead of him on the success ladder.

She mentally shuddered. Without a doubt he'd try to remake Deke in his image—an intolerable option. Just what the office—no, make that the world—didn't need was another walking, talking penis.

Between the tingle along her neck and the Lyle factor, she made a swift, sure decision.

"Okay. I'll do it. I'll repackage you."

LATER THAT DAY, after work, Deke whistled tunelessly as he ambled down the sidewalk toward the pub where he and Abby were meeting to finalize their plans. The naked, bare branches of the trees had begun to boast buds that would soon explode in a pink profusion. Washington, D.C.'s cherry blossoms were legendary.

The evening chill had taken on a different quality. A subtle, underlying warmth heralded the arrival of Spring. A change of seasons. A rebirth of nature. A rebirth of Deke. He was absolutely sure of it because he'd solicited the best.

Deke would've never approached Lyle Turner, primarily because he couldn't stand the guy. But he'd known the mention of Lyle would turn the tide for him with Abby. He might be a geek, but he wasn't a dumb geek.

Up ahead, he saw the shingled sign for O'Donaghel's Chew and Brew pub. Ducking into the doorway, the aroma of stout ale and corned beef greeted him like a long-lost friend. He always found O'Donaghels welcoming with it's stamped tin ceiling, aged brick walls, and scarred wooden floors. Laughter and conversation, hallmarks of O'Donaghels in full happy-hour mode, vied with the rousing traditional Irish music played over the speakers.

Deke spotted Abby immediately. She sat jotting down notes in an open book, ignoring the rest of the room. He supposed Abby qualified as more interesting than pretty with her heart-shaped face and nearly translucent skin that contrasted with her short dark hair. Then there were those large silver, magical eyes.

A guy at the bar was watching her as if he was working up the nerve to say something. Deke shot him a territorial look and pulled out the chair next to her. If he sat across the table, they'd never hear one another over the noise.

She glanced up, her silvery-gray eyes sparkling, and nodded in greeting. "Deke."

"Hi." He settled into the chair and his knee bumped against hers. The brief contact sent heat ricocheting through him. "Sorry." A quick waitress took his drink order, saving the moment from awkwardness. She glanced at Abby, "Another seltzer for you?"

Abby shook her head. "I'm fine, thanks." She switched her attention back to Deke and said something. He saw her lips move and heard the murmur of her voice but couldn't make out her words.

He shook his head and leaned forward, "I'm sorry. I

can't hear you." She leaned in as well, close enough that he could see dark flecks in her silver eyes that turned them to molten steel and smell her scent of musk and cinnamon and spices that evoked exotic places. "I thought O'Donaghels would be a good place to meet since I've never seen anyone from MCL in here."

Deke was pleased with the choice because he was familiar with the pub and would feel more comfortable here—a home turf advantage if you will. "Do you want to go somewhere else? Someplace less noisy?" he asked.

"No." Her breath stirred against his jaw and he forced himself to focus on the conversation rather than the fullness of her mouth mere inches from his own. "At least here, no one's likely to eavesdrop. I've roughed out some things we need to go over before we begin. Do you still want to do this."

"I do."

She nodded and then plowed forward. "What exactly do you want to accomplish?"

Hadn't they covered this earlier? "What do you mean?"

"Do you just want to get to the point where you can line up a date or do you want to become a player?"

"A player?" He couldn't contain a snort of laughter. "Let's get real, Abby. We're still talking about me. No, I don't foresee being a player."

She flashed an answering grin at him, amusement sparkling in her eyes, laughing *with* him, not *at* him. For a second shared camaraderie bound them, then Abby seemed to remember herself and the grin vanished.

"Okay. We'll mark off becoming a player wannabe." She scribbled in her notebook. "So what do you want? Serious professional? *GQ* hip? Sophisticated man-about-town? Rugged outdoorsman?"

How the heck was he supposed to know? "I guess I'll need your help on that too."

The waitress arrived with his beer. Deke took a swallow of the dark draft while Abby made further notations. She put down her pen and nursed her seltzer.

"How much are you willing to put into this?" Her silver eyes pinned him.

He put the mug on the table. They hadn't yet discussed her fee. "Money's no object. The sky's the limit. Name your fee."

She shook her head impatiently. "I'm not talking about money. I'm talking about you. How much of yourself are you willing to give to this project?"

"Everything. I'm willing to give one hundred and ten percent."

"What kind of timeline are we looking at?"

"As soon as possible."

She made a notation in her notebook and then put down her pen, turning the full force of those eyes of hers on him again. "I need to know one thing—why is this so important to you? Why the sudden urgency?" She tilted her head to one side, a small frown wrinkling her brow. "You've looked like this for as long as we've worked together," she said dispassionately.

He rubbed his finger along the side of the mug,

tracing a pattern in the frosted glass. "A couple of months ago my best friend Greg died in an auto accident. I've been doing a lot of thinking and I've realized I'm wasting my life."

Sympathy warmed her eyes and something inside him shifted. But pity wasn't what he wanted from her. "I wouldn't say you've wasted your life. You have an important job that you're very good at."

"Thank you. But Greg's death made me realize there's more to life than work. I've known that but I always thought I'd do something about it tomorrow." He shrugged. "Except tomorrow isn't always ours." He snared her gaze and bared his soul. "My house used to feel comfortable, now it just feels lonely."

Abby's eyes widened as she pursed her lips, and for a moment he glimpsed an acknowledgment, an understanding, as if she too had walked that path. "Okay. Fair enough. Do you have anyone in mind or do you just want a make-over before putting yourself out there?"

He felt as awkward as a teenager with a crush. He shoved his glasses up onto the bridge of his nose. "There is someone I'm…I'd like to…I'm interested in someone." He finally managed to get it out.

Abby quirked an eyebrow at him. "And what's she like?"

"She's great—smart, sexy, successful." He'd say that described Abby to a *T*.

She shot him a skeptical look. "Successful doesn't seem to appeal to most men."

"I'm not most men."

Her expression remained noncommittal but there was a glimmer of something…. "No, you're not. Have you tried asking her out?"

"No."

"Well, maybe you should just try asking her out first."

"I don't think so. I met her when I first moved to D.C." He'd felt Abby's impact the first time he'd laid eyes on her. "She…uh, barely notices I'm alive." In the year that he'd worked with her, she hadn't spared him a second glance. But Greg's death had been a wake-up call. Deke was a desperate man and that called for desperate measures. He needed Abby to make him over—for her. He wasn't exactly lying, but he wasn't exactly throwing the truth out on the table. If he told her *she* was the woman he wanted, she'd get up and walk out the door and that would be the end of that. "Statistically I stand a much better chance of her saying yes after my repackaging."

Her gaze swept over him and he flinched at the unadorned truth in her look. "Well, there is that." He'd have to hand it to Abby—at least she didn't dole out false platitudes.

"As my Grandma used to say, I'm burning daylight. I want to get this done as soon as possible. I was thinking in the next two weeks. I'd like to ask her to the picnic." MCL's idea of corporate bonding was an annual spring picnic where employees brought their families and Melvin Mansell, one of the partners, always amazed them by manning the grill and not getting burned in the process. "I thought the picnic might be a good place to start."

"That's tough, but doable. We'll need to work nights and weekends to get you ready. I need to observe you outside of the office. If we both take some time off—"

"Time off?" This was more than he'd hoped for.

"As I indicated earlier, it would be very intensive. First, I'd spend some time observing you while you go about your everyday business. Next we'd develop a plan. Then we'd implement it. This is more than just a costume change. And when you repackage a product, it may go in stages, but it's not revealed to the public until it's a 'fait accompli.'"

"Don't you think there might be some talk around the office if we're both out on vacation at the same time?"

"Do you really think people would pair the two of us together?" *Ouch*. Even though he didn't think she meant it *that* way. "I don't believe we have anything in common and we've never shown any interest in one another."

True enough, they'd never shown an iota of interest in one another. He hadn't had the nerve and well…she didn't have any interest. There'd be no gossip.

"I'll put in my vacation request tomorrow."

She closed her day planner. "Fine. So will I. I have some preliminary things to pull together so we'll begin work this weekend." She glanced at her watch. "Sorry to run, but I need to get home to my dog." She pulled out her wallet and he motioned for her to put it away.

"I've got it." She opened her mouth and he was certain it was to argue. He forestalled her. "Just factor it into your fee."

She stood and smiled, a genuine, unguarded moment, and his heart flip-flopped inside his chest. "Goodnight, Abby."

"Goodnight, Deke. Thanks."

She wove her way through O'Doneghals without a backward glance.

Two weeks. He had two weeks to convince Abby he was the man for her. He had his work cut out for him.

CHAPTER TWO

TWO EVENINGS LATER, Abby pulled a few strands of blonde hair through the frosting cap and passed a hand-held mirror to Margo Simmons, her next-door neighbor and good friend. "What do you think? More in the front or is that okay?"

Margo eyed herself critically. "Looks good to me." She turned her head to the right and squinted into the hand mirror. "Do you think my eyelids are drooping? That runs in my family, you know." She laid the mirror back on the kitchen table as if she couldn't bear to look.

Abby topped off their margarita glasses, sipped and checked out Margo's bright blue eyes. The halogen track lighting in Margo's kitchen hid nothing. There wasn't the slightest droop to her lids. "You're certifiably insane. There's nothing wrong with your eyes. And how can you even think about your eyes when you've got that cap on your head sprouting strands of hair all over the place? Every time we do this I think you look like an alien." Why Margo didn't go to the salon to get her hair foiled like every other blonde in the world was beside her. But Margo liked the cap, so they did the cap.

"Yeah, well, I may look like an alien, but I'm not moving in with Deke the Geek," Margo needled her.

Abby traded her margarita glass for the plastic bottle of hair solution and dumped it into the plastic tray with the powder. "Behave, Margo. Don't antagonize the woman in charge of your hair color…unless you want to join the circus. You know good and well I'm not moving in with him." Margo had a tendency to embellish a story. "And *I* didn't call him Deke the Geek." She'd thought it…but she hadn't said it.

"Maybe you'll get laid." Margo slanted Abby an arch look. Margo loved to play the outrageous card and Abby reciprocated by not reacting.

"I'll admit it's been a while, but Deke?" Now why'd she automatically picture his dark eyes and start to feel sort of warm inside? She squelched that image and focused instead on his shaggy hair and his nervous habit of shoving at his glasses. "Perish the thought. No thank you." She mixed the color with the little wand until the gel and powder formed a paste. "Keep talking like that and you'll get platinum highlights," she threatened sweetly. "Pull your mind out of the gutter."

"It's in the bedroom," Margo smirked, "not the gutter."

"Anyway, Deke's the one looking to get laid," Abby said, as she worked the thick, goopy mess through the strands of hair sticking out of the cap. "Actually, the poor, delusional man wants to get married."

"Hmm," her friend murmured speculatively.

"No. Capital *N*, capital *O*. You're barking up the

wrong tree." Abby snapped the plastic bonnet in place and set the microwave timer. "And he's got someone all picked out. You should've seen the look in his eye when he described her." For a moment, an unexpected longing had pierced her, a yearning to have someone look like that when he thought of *her*. She'd snuffed out that notion in its fragile infancy.

She tossed the left over hair color in the garbage and carefully peeled off the rubber gloves that came in the kit. Abby plopped back into the kitchen chair and re-claimed her glass.

"Well, in that case, I can see why he wouldn't want to marry you. But that doesn't rule out the horizontal delight."

"I'm not interested in—as you so colorfully phrased it—doing the horizontal delight with Deke." Just because he had nice eyes and smelled good and she'd felt a moment of…well, something that she didn't want to examine too closely when she'd met him at O'Don-eghals and his leg had pressed against hers, it hadn't been repellent at all.

"You should be," Margo retorted.

What Margo didn't know wouldn't hurt her and it would make Abby's life infinitely easier to keep those errant thoughts to herself. "Just because you and Shawn are happily married sex addicts doesn't mean we all have to be." She'd met the couple when she'd bought her condo and moved next door after her divorce. Aside from the occasional spat, Shawn and Margo were still in love and couldn't seem to get enough of one another.

They were definitely the exception in Abby's realm of experience, probably because Shawn, a management consultant, traveled more than he was home.

"What—happily married or sex addicts?"

"Both. Either. Besides, you don't even know the man." Margo's earlier insult came to mind. "And exactly why wouldn't someone want to marry me?"

Margo leveled her a *get real* look. "Maybe because you've got a rotten attitude about marriage."

"Rotten, no. Realistic, yes." First Carley, now Margo.

"But getting laid," Margo continued, "you're the perfect candidate."

Irreverent, out-there Margo always made her laugh with her convoluted logic. Abby sipped from her margarita. "I'm sure I'll regret this, but I'll bite—why am I the perfect candidate for sex?"

"One word and it starts with an *R*. Take a guess."

Abby pretended to ponder it for a moment. "Realistic? Reactive? Receptive? Restless?" Wait a minute. Where had that restless come from? She wasn't restless in the least. Was she?

"No." Margo smirked. "Repressed."

"Repressed? Hardly." Abby offered a dry laugh.

"Repressed. As in you need to cut loose. Have a little fun. Make a little whoopee. And your geek could probably use the practice." Margo slanted her an arch look. "Aren't you gonna turn him into a hunk? This is heady stuff. Just think—you've got a man ready, willing and able to change. You have the opportunity to create the perfect man. *Your* perfect man." Margo widened her baby blues. "If you're up to the job."

Abby recognized manipulation when she heard it, but that recognition didn't lessen the impact. "I'm up to the job. But it doesn't mean I want to sleep with him. And Deke Foster wouldn't be my perfect man. *The perfect man* is another one of those modern myths, right along with *'til death do we part* and *happy ever after*. It doesn't exist."

"Regardless, he's gonna need some practice. Honey, you can't just slap a new set of clothes on him and turn him loose. He'll fall flat on his face."

She knew that and had planned accordingly. "I have thought about that." Margo arched an eyebrow suggestively. Abby shook her head. "Not the horizontal delight but the practice. He needs a few dating dry runs to get his confidence up before he approaches his true love. We don't want him botching this." And she considered his success with his target woman part and parcel of the make-over. When a repackaged product was launched, if it didn't garner the target marketshare, she hadn't successfully done her job.

Margo bobbed her head in agreement. "Miss Congeniality?" Margo owned the DVD. "Like when she looks good all made over but then she opens her mouth."

"Exactly. And since I'm not in the least attracted to him—" her reaction to those eyes didn't count…well, not for much "—and he's not interested in me…well, I'll be the perfect practice partner for him."

"A little practice wouldn't hurt you either. Maybe it'll get you warmed up for when Mr. Right drops into your life." Abby didn't bother to argue. "What's the next step in turning your ugly duckling into a hot swan, Leda?"

Abby also ignored the reference to the mythical Leda and the Swan. "Well, to make sure I don't slap the inappropriate packaging on him, I've put together a questionnaire for him to fill out that lets me know something about him. It's a critical step with my consumer products clients."

"Yeah, toots, except he's a man, not a tube of toothpaste or a bar of soap."

"So? Theoretically it works the same. I repackage him and help him pull together a marketing plan, we dry run it and if we're successful, he probably gets his woman."

"There's only one problem there."

She didn't see a problem at all. "What?"

"Chemistry. There's got to be chemistry between them."

Abby shrugged. "That's one of those factors I can't control. I can, however, work with him so he can maximize his chemistry-generating potential."

"And you're doing this by having him fill out a consumer products questionnaire?"

"Of course not. I surfed a couple of those on-line dating sites and compiled a questionnaire based on their criteria."

"Now we're talking." Margo's eyes sparkled. "Cool. I want to see it. I've got another fifteen minutes on my hair. Go get it and I'll mix another pitcher of margaritas."

Why not? Abby left Margo measuring and to run quickly next door. Margo found the strangest things interesting. But then Margo was a bit of a law unto herself.

Abby returned as Margo finished mixing and exchanged the sheaf of papers for a fresh glass.

Margo thumbed through it and wrinkled her nose. "This is sort of boring. Where's the juicy sex stuff?"

The timer went off, signaling the next step of the hair processing event. Abby laughed and turned on the water in the sink until it ran tepid. "You have a one-track mind. There's no juicy sex stuff because that's not the kind of information I need."

Margo, never satisfied unless she got in the last word, corrected her. "You are so wrong. It's the juicy sex stuff that's going to tell you what you really need to know about your man." She was still smirking when Abby plunged her head beneath the running water.

CHAPTER THREE

"FINALLY," ABBY GRUMBLED to Mini, who was sitting in the front seat next to her, as she backed up and eased into the tight parallel parking space. "I hope you appreciate my sacrifice of driving through traffic to get here so you could come too. It would've been so much easier to catch the metro and hop off at McPherson Square. But since you're not allowed on the subway you'd have been stuck home alone. I hope you appreciate this." It just hadn't seemed right to leave Mini at home considering how much time the dog spent alone already. And Deke hadn't seemed to mind when Abby had suggested bringing her dog along with her.

Minerva pranced over and licked Abby's arm in appreciation. Well, perhaps not appreciation, because Minerva was always looking for any reason to lick but unlike many Chihuahuas she wasn't a barker. Abby'd take licking over barking any day.

Abby retrieved her briefcase, snapped on Minerva's retractable leash, and climbed out of the car. Traffic might've sucked—when didn't traffic suck in D.C.— and she'd had to backtrack when she realized she'd left the questionnaire at Margo's after one too many margaritas. Now she was now running late, but it was still a gorgeous morning. The sun shone, white cotton-candy clouds dotted a blue sky, and in the past month the last vestiges of dirty snow had disappeared.

Mini minced along, slightly ahead of Abby, as if she owned the sidewalk. Nice area. Very nice. Historic row houses, some brick, some stucco, a few stone, but all echoing the grace and charm of a bygone era, lined both sides of the street. She paused as she passed a wrought-iron fence that abutted the sidewalk and checked the number on the next house. Yep, this was it.

The house, three stories with a daylight basement, was a warm, dark redbrick. Gray brick and stone, along with pediments contributed architectural interest, as did the three-storied bay window, with fourth floor dormers. Two gleaming black doors topped by a glass transom stood at the top of a short flight of broad stone stairs. Elegance without pretension came to mind.

"Nice digs, eh, Mini?" She scooped the little dog up, tucked her under one arm, and mounted the stairs. She buzzed Deke on the call box mounted by the front doors and he answered her almost immediately.

"Sure, I'll be right down."

Abby started. She'd noticed the other night, for the first time, what a nice voice he had—a rich, smooth baritone that brought to mind tangled sheets and wicked phrases whispered in the dark of the night.

She'd probably never noticed it before because the

majority of her interaction with Deke at the office had been through the occasional e-mail or at a meeting where his nervous habit of pushing at his glasses and his dubious fashion sense proved so distracting.

That voice was a real asset. Whew! He'd sounded pretty darn sexy just uttering those words. Imagine what he could do to a woman's heat index when she taught him the right phrases to murmur in that sexy voice.

She looked into Mini's big eyes. "So far, so good, Min. I've come up with two assets. Nice eyes and a nice voice. We're making progress."

Deke threw open the door and two sets of puppy dog brown eyes welcomed them. The canine variety belonged to a Boxer with a massive head and a lean, muscular body that quivered with repressed excitement. The dog gave one short woof, definitely a greeting rather than a warning, and sat, its long, pink tongue lolling out of its enormous mouth.

Shifting from one foot to the other, Deke shoved his glasses up the bridge of his nose. "Hi." He sounded as nervous as he looked. Although Abby had to say, nervous or not, he looked better in worn jeans and a long-sleeved MIT sweatshirt that hung on him than he ever had in his work clothes. At least nothing clashed. "Come in." He moved and stumbled into the dog, catching himself against the wall. Oh brother. For whatever progress they'd made, they still had a long way to go.

Abby slipped past him into the foyer. A vintage chandelier hung suspended from what was at least a twelve-foot ceiling. A narrow staircase hugged the left wall. Deke closed the door behind her and she caught a whiff of his scent. Yet one more thing they didn't have to work on. He smelled good. Nothing overwhelming, just a hint of sensual scent that made a woman yearn to get closer.

He turned to her and smiled, but it wasn't directed at Abby. "You must be Minerva." He sent a questioning glance Abby's way, obviously seeking permission to pet Minerva.

"Sure," she said.

He held out his hand. Mini sniffed delicately and then granted him an approving lick. Deke laughed softly and scratched behind Mini's ear, which brought his hand in extremely close proximity to Abby's right breast.

"Oh. You're a sweetie aren't you?" Deke crooned in a low tone that sent heat spiraling through Abby. Uh-huh. That was the perfect voice, pitch, tone…whatever…for pillow talk. "I bet you run the house, don't you?"

He looked at Abby, his earlier awkwardness forgotten thanks to Mini, his brown eyes alight with teasing. When he relaxed and smiled like that he was really quite…well, attractive despite his bad haircut and untrimmed beard.

Abby laughed, her voice coming out breathless and edgy. "Very perceptive. You've got Mini's number."

He smiled and her stomach did a slow somersault. "It's this way," he said, pausing at the foot of the stairs to allow her to go first. "Third floor walk-up, but only two sets of stairs because of the basement." A carpeted stair runner muffled their footsteps. "By the way, this is Mac. He may look fierce, but he's really a big baby. He'll be fine with Minerva."

Abby laughed and rubbed her thumb against Mini's chest. "Nice to meet you Mac," she said to the dog. "Mini may look like a baby, but she's really a terror." She turned back to Deke. "I'll hold on to her while she meets Mac, just to make sure she behaves. And thanks again for letting her come."

Climbing behind her, Deke chuckled. "No problem. No reason for her to sit home alone while you're here."

They climbed the second flight of stairs in silence except for the occasional click of Mac's toenails on the wood stair outside the runner, Abby incredibly aware of Deke behind her. Her breath quickened. If she was honest she'd admit it wasn't simply the exertion of climbing stairs that was making her breathing difficult. Deke's voice and clean masculine scent wrapped around her from behind and set her pulse tripping.

But he was a geek—*and* a project. She shouldn't care, because she wasn't interested in him personally but she couldn't help wondering if her jeans made her butt looked too wide from behind.

"This is it," Deke said as they reached the next landing. He opened the door. Mac, obviously glad to be home after his brief trip downstairs, charged past them in the narrow hall, knocking Deke into Abby.

One second he was beside her, the next he was plastered against her, his arms wrapped around her, one hand clutching her backside. He quickly righted himself, but not before she'd noted the strength in his arms, the lean hard line of his body, the intoxication of his scent, the tickle of his warm breath against her neck and a blast of furnace heat when he'd grabbed her ass. Mini issued a low growl—either due to being squeezed or territorial regarding Abby or both—and within seconds Deke released her. Abby blinked. Deke Foster had just flipped her switch.

She reminded herself why she was here and busied herself looking around. A quick glance revealed hardwood floors, comfortable furniture that reminded her of one of those turn of the century exclusive men's clubs—clubby leather chairs with a large ottoman, a sprawling leather couch, a multi-colored rug that looked more Turkish than Oriental. Altogether it bespoke traditional masculine power. Considering the way he dressed himself for work, it wasn't what she expected. "Very nice," she said, nodding to Deke who was still by the door.

A dull red painted his neck and the parts of his face not covered by facial hair. He finally seemed to find his voice. "Oh. God. I'm so sorry. He gets excited sometimes. I didn't mean to grab your…I would've never…I mean…I'm really sorry."

Dear God. She could clean him up. Get him a decent haircut, but if blushed like a Victorian virgin every time he bumped into a woman, he was never going to get anywhere. And that was not acceptable, because she didn't fail at projects. And when it came down to the bottom line, that's exactly what Deke Foster was—a project. And she'd repackage him successfully, regardless of what it took. Right now, it looked like honesty was the best policy.

"Deke, stop. You've got to relax. Until you turned all red and started to apologize, well…I liked it."

CHAPTER FOUR

"YOU LIKED IT?" He still vividly remembered the look in her eyes when she'd first thought he was interested in her. Not exactly encouraging.

She smiled, her eyes more silver than gray and his gut tightened. She had no clue how just a smile rocked his world. "Yeah. It wasn't as if you were groping me or trying to cop a feel. Mac knocked you off-kilter and you wound up grabbing my…uh…well, me."

Despite her rational approach, she seemed a bit flustered, or maybe it just looked that way to him because his heart was still racing. Regardless, she took a moment to let Minerva down. She and Mac did the traditional dog sniff thing and when it was apparent the two liked one another, Abby leaned down to unleash the Chihuahua, offering him a delectable view of the jean-clad bottom he'd so recently grabbed. Deke swallowed hard. She straightened and Mac and Mini trotted off to the back of the house.

"They seem to have hit it off," he said, desperate to talk about something other than him flailing around and grabbing her butt. He was fairly certain the kind of man that attracted Abby didn't have two left feet.

Abby laughed, "Thank God. It makes it much easier to get things done. Now let's get started. One of the things we're going to work on is the way you present yourself." Damn it, he knew it. "But we'll get around to that later. Why don't you try to relax and show me your place. Let me get to know you."

Deke almost laughed. Relaxing while she got to know him struck him as mutually exclusive, especially with her curves still imprinted against his body like a brand. And he'd never seen her in a pair of jeans. She wore them well. He'd have to have been blind not to notice the way the soft denim hugged her hips and her round bottom as she'd climbed the stairs ahead of him. But he'd committed to making this change and as she'd proven a couple of days ago, she wouldn't hesitate to walk out if she didn't think he was fully committed. So he'd do his damnedest to forget the disconcerting sexy memory of her bottom in those jeans. "Sure. I'll relax and show you around. No problem."

Obviously he sounded less than convincing. "Look. What do feel the most comfortable with? Programming codes?"

"Yeah. I'd say that's pretty much it."

"Okay. Try this. Think of me as a component in a new software program you're working on. Or better yet think of me as the beta test. I'm here to help you work out the glitches in your system so your program runs at its full capacity. Smooth, efficient."

There was definitely something wrong with him,

because for some reason, that struck him as really sexy. Of course he was in such a sorry state, and had been since the first time he'd laid eyes on her when she'd marched into a meeting with her short skirt and stiletto heels. She'd owned him from the get-go. He was a man versed in logic and it was supremely illogical to ascribe to love at first sight. Madness really. But it had been a year and she still owned him, even though he'd worked with her enough to know she was stubborn verging on intractable. Nor was she long on patience. And yes, he was in a sorry state indeed when even thinking of her as a beta test got him all worked up. It just proved what a hopelessly geeky guy he was. God help him if she mentioned his hard drive. "You're the beta test that's going to make me run smooth?"

"Exactly. I'm the beta and if it makes you feel any better, I'll think of you as a bar of soap."

Abby definitely thought outside the box. And he definitely didn't. "I'm not sure I follow."

"You're a commodity—like a bar of soap. It's my job to repackage you to maximize your potential in the marketplace—your particular market being women and more specifically this one woman you want. So, while some of this may feel personal, it's really not."

That was an interesting insight into Abby's mind. Rather convoluted if you asked him and he was damn sure he didn't like being thought of as a bar of soap. But if that's what got her here and that's what would keep her here, turning him into the man she'd want then he'd go with the flowchart…uh, the flow. "Okay, this way Madam Beta." She grinned at him and oddly enough, he did feel more relaxed, simply because Abby seemed to find him mildly funny as opposed to overwhelmingly geeky.

He took her on a quick tour of the den, galley kitchen, dining room, to the doorway of his bedroom which overlooked the street and then back through the house to the other end. "This is very nice. Did you pick out the furnishings yourself?" She couldn't quite mask the note of surprise.

"Kind of. A designer at the furniture store helped me. I told her what I liked and what I wanted and she sort of put things together for me."

"The results are beautiful. I love it."

Deke mentally heaved a sigh of relief. He'd picked chocolate browns and creams for the most part. The designer had said it was elegant in vogue. He'd just known he liked it. It felt calm and relaxing to him. But he'd wondered if Abby would think his place too conservative, too stuffy, too, well, boring.

He ushered her into the second bedroom on the other side of the den. "This was a second bedroom with a bathroom. The house is an ideal set-up for roommates. But I don't have a roommate and since my infrequent guests aren't overnighters and I prefer to work in a room with windows, I made this into my office." Minerva and Mac lay curled up together, sharing Mac's dog bed in a sunny spot next to the door that opened to a deck off the back.

Abby walked in behind him and brushed past, not quite touching him, but close enough that he caught his breath at the citrus scent that clung to her hair and skin.

"At least he's keeping her out of trouble," Abby said, eyeing the two dogs.

"I think Mac's glad of the canine companionship. I think sometimes he gets lonely."

"Apparently Mini was too. I guess everyone needs someone now and then." For a brief second he glimpsed a shadow in her silver eyes that attested to her own loneliness. She shrugged off the moment it happened and glanced at his desk, seeing all the technical equipment she'd obviously expected. But it was his weights on the other side of the room that seemed to capture her attention. She looked at him and it became his turn to shrug self-consciously. "My dad had a heart attack when I was in high school. A combination of stress, being overweight and having poor eating habits. It was only logical that I take the necessary steps not to do the same."

"How often do you work out?" she asked.

He shrugged again. "Five to seven days a week. It's a habit."

She looked at him, as if assessing him beneath his clothes, and he pretty much felt as if she was looking at a bar of soap. "Are you hiding a great body under clothes a size too large?"

"My clothes are comfortable," he said. "I'm in decent shape, but no, I wouldn't say great."

If someone had asked what was the last thing you

expected quiet, shy, geeky Deke Foster to do, somewhere at the top of that list would've been to take off his T-shirt and toss it onto the weight bench. Maybe he was caught up in the moment of finding a new him. Maybe it was because Abby looked at him as if he was soap rather than flesh and blood. Maybe he was thrown off track by the slant of her silver eyes and the bewitching way her hair curled over her right ear. Whatever the crazy impetus that overtook him, Deke decided to go with it. Pulling his shirt over his head, he tossed it onto the weight bench. "But here, you judge for yourself."

Cool air kissed his bare upper body. Abby's silver gaze slid over him and he seemed to heat from the inside out. A delicate flush tinged her skin pink.

Something primal surfaced within him, a powerful force that liked the way she looked at him. He wasn't a virgin, so it wasn't as if he'd never taken his shirt off in front of a woman. And it wasn't as if a woman had never eyed him with a measure of appreciation. But to have *Abby* look at him this way…. Their eyes caught and held, snared in a tension that sprang up between a semi-dressed man and a woman very aware of him.

She cleared her throat, breaking the moment and pulling him back to reality. "You can put your shirt back on. I've seen enough."

His usual self-consciousness engulfed him once again as he pulled on his shirt. "Okay. So, that's the house. What do we do now?" God, he was a helpless dork. "I…uh…mean, what's the next step?"

CHAPTER FIVE

ABBY SUCKED IN a deep breath and scrambled for her usual equanimity, which had definitely gone missing in action when Deke pulled off his shirt. Mother of God, he had a body that would send most normal women over the edge.

And he hadn't just been coy—he really, truly didn't seem to know what an incredibly hunky body he possessed.

Sculpted, lean muscles defined a broad chest, shoulders and arms. In the two-seconds it'd taken for him to whip off that shirt, he'd gone from Deke the Geek to Deke her own Roman gladiator. Move over Russell Crowe.

And she still felt all flushed and hot and bothered. It was ridiculous for her to react this way. She was a professional and he was just another product. This wasn't personal. She was just vulnerable to the situation right now, what with all the talk of being lonely. This was about the situation, not Deke. And she'd prove it to herself.

"On second thought. Why don't you slip off your pants and your shirt too, so I know what I'm working with."

"You want me to strip down to my underwear? I really don't think that's such a good idea."

She wasn't being voyeuristic—she just needed to prove to herself that she could be immune to him, that he was just another job. She smiled and she knew it held a hint of condescension. "Deke, I assure you, I'm not being a pervert. It's part of my process. I take a product and strip it down to its barest essence and then I go from there. I have a brother and I've been married before. I have seen a male in his underwear once or twice." She lifted her shoulders and let them drop. "Remember, you're a bar of soap. That's how I'm thinking of you." Well, that wasn't exactly true. She was *trying* to think of him as a bar of soap. But it wasn't working as well as she'd hoped.

Something flashed in his dark eyes and a smile she'd never seen before tugged at his lips. A smile that set her heart beating a little faster than normal because it was sexy and edgy and maybe just a little angry. "Sure. A bar of soap. Why not, then?" Her pulse leapt.

He took a step closer, never taking his eyes off her. Deke pulled the shirt over his head once again and dropped it to the floor. Still not looking away, he unbuttoned his jeans and slid the zipper down. The sound seemed to reverberate in the room's quiet. He slid the denim over his hips and let them drop. Abby's breath caught, trapped in her chest.

He stepped forward, out of the jeans pooled around his feet. *Bar of soap. Bar of soap.* Distance Abby. Keep a mental distance. He hooked his thumbs in the waistband of his boxers. "These too?"

"No," she managed to utter through a totally dry

mouth. Because every drop of moisture in her body had headed south and was now pooled between her legs.

If he'd been hot without the shirt, he was a flaming inferno standing before her in nothing but plaid boxers. Abby's grandfather had been a woodworker. Deke's skin gleamed like oak with a honey gold finish. She'd seen guys at the beach and at the pool which had nice upper bodies, but also had scrawny legs or were sometimes too beefy. That wasn't the case with Deke. His thighs, lean, muscular, with just the right amount of dark hair, were just as perfect and symmetrical as the rest of his body…well, the parts that she could see. And her imagination, which was usually dead and buried, was now alive and well and filling in the blanks beneath the boxers.

Suddenly the room felt too small, the air between them too charged. She wanted to look anywhere but at him but couldn't seem to take her eyes off him. Something flickered in his dark eyes. He took a step closer and Abby leaned back, causing the frame of the door to press against her.

"And this is what the soap looks like from the other side," Deke said, turning around, presenting her with a wall of masculine back, a trim waist, and boxers that were riding low on sexy hips.

"Okay. Thank you." She was proud of how steady her voice came out. Maybe it was an octave lower and a shade huskier and not quite as crisp and business-like as she might've liked, but still, she was in control.

He turned to face her. "Are you sure? Didn't you want me stripped to my barest essence? Are you sure you really know what you're working with? Don't you want to touch me? I'm not being a pervert or anything, I just want to get my money's worth and make sure you do your job." He tossed her words back at her and his eyes issued a challenge.

Was he toying with her? Could he tell how his near-nakedness affected her pulse rate, not to mention other body parts? Did he think she was scared to touch him? As for what he was paying her, she'd definitely give him his money's worth.

"By all means, I should definitely touch you." Abby reached up and skimmed her hand over his shoulder and down his arm. His skin sent heat flooding through her and warning bells clamoring in her head. Instead of heeding the warning, she did the last thing she'd ever expect herself to do. Made reckless by the heat so unfamiliar to her, she touched him yet again. She slid her fingers back up his arm, trailing them over the curve of his bicep that, quite frankly, sent a thrill through her and over his chest, feeling the mold of muscle and the stark sensuality of bare skin and masculine hair beneath her fingertips. And still she continued her exploration, down the broad plane to the flat landscape of his belly to the band of his underwear. He sucked in a rasping breath and it harmonized with the ragged edge of her breathing.

Deke reached between them and snared her hand. His blunt, well-shaped fingers encircled her wrist. "That's enough. You may think of me as a bar of soap, but, and I suppose you'll have to trust me on this, I'm a man."

His touch, the low sensual quality of his voice and his words, his scent, the warmth of his skin, all fired along her synapses, inciting an erotic riot inside her. He stepped closer still, causing her brain to check out and her body to check in, registering the tantalizing proximity of his near nakedness.

"If this is a five senses reconnaissance mission, you need the whole picture. You know how I sound, how I look, how I feel, how I smell…" He lowered his head, giving her ample time to protest, to run, to…damn it, do something other than stand there and wallow in the pleasure of his fingers wrapped around her wrist, his masculine scent, his close proximity, enjoying the heat skittering through her in anticipation of what she knew was coming. He braced his other hand on the wall, effectively pinning her in. Her heart raced. She was positively drowning in the eat-it-now-and-you'll-regret-it-later dark chocolate of his eyes. "Now this is how I taste."

There was nothing tentative or unsure in his kiss. His mouth descended on hers in a hot drugging kiss that unleashed a reciprocal torrent of want and need from somewhere deep inside her. His tongue probed at the seam of her lips and she opened herself to him, hungry for the passion she was tasting. In the end it was Deke who came to his senses and pulled away.

Immediately she withdrew her hand from his neck

and dragged her eyes away from the temptation lurking in his. She looked somewhere past his shoulder to gather her thoughts.

This was Deke Foster, geek extraordinaire. She tugged her hand free of his.

He was immediately contrite. "I'm sorry, Abby." He shoved his hand through his hair, standing it on end, which should have made him look geeky. Maybe he did, but also came across as disconcertingly sexy on the heels of that kiss. Still, despite the hunger he'd aroused in her, she needed to put this in perspective—for both of them.

"No. That was perfect. The Deke Foster I know would've never initiated a kiss like that. That was an excellent exercise in thinking of me as a beta test."

Abby didn't realize she'd been quietly holding her breath until he stepped into his jeans, tugged them up over his hips and zipped them into place.

Couldn't he have been soft and flabby or at least faintly repulsive instead of mouthwateringly yummy? She told herself not to be an imbecile. He was a veritable physical gold mine beneath those baggy clothes. As a project manager, she couldn't have asked for more.

"You mean you're not upset that I kissed you?" he asked.

"Of course not." She walked over to the window and looked out at the deck that lay beyond the French doors. Despite the hunger and the heat, their kiss didn't mean anything. He wanted his dream woman and she…well, it had simply been a long time. In the scheme of things, what was some casual physical contact? Ultimately nothing to her, but it might make the difference between success and failure to the project. "Role play is important."

He tugged his T-shirt over his head and she breathed a deeper sigh of relief. "I mean, it's not as if you're attracted to me and conversely you're not my type…so I think we could just put what just happened down to an anomaly."

His dark eyes were unreadable. "Nothing happened. You were checking me out for the project." He ushered her out of the weight room, his touch light and impersonal at her elbow, his tone even and non-committal. Why then did that brief brush of his fingers against her elbow send her pulse into overdrive?

"So, what's next? Where do we go from here?"

How about a room with a lot of space between them where she could check the Lost and Found for her mind, which had obviously wandered off while she wasn't watching? "I've got a questionnaire for you. It covers a variety of topics. Don't give the questions too much thought—that's why I didn't e-mail it to you. I'm looking for gut responses. I need to know what you're all about so I can make sure that the packaging reflects the man inside."

"And what if it already does?"

No way. Geek or not, she'd just discovered he was hot. "Don't worry about it. Just fill it out. That will give me a much better idea of what I'm working with."

A bar of soap. Right.

DEKE SAT BY THE FIREPLACE, flipped over the sheet of paper, and attempted to focus on the questionnaire in front of him instead of the way Abby had felt in his arms, the way she'd returned his kiss. Thing were going much better than he'd dreamed and he wasn't about to kill any progress he'd made by stalling out because he was daydreaming about the pillowy softness of her lips. Great tacticians didn't relax and proclaim victory when one battle went their way. No, they persevered and pressed on until they'd won the war. Abby had kissed him back, and the memory still left him flushed and wanting. But she'd also put it down to mere practice, which meant the war wasn't over. Still, she'd left the field wide open for more practice. So, for now he'd adhere to her rules of engagement. He dragged his mind back from the thought of her mouth, hot and ripe beneath his, to the questionnaire at hand.

Abby hadn't been kidding when she said she had a questionnaire for him to fill out. Six pages and four more to go. So far, on paper, he'd shared his preference for healthy food, although he did have a thing for little white powdered doughnuts, scary movies, the beach rather than the mountains and live theater rather than movies.

And now he was at the sex section. He didn't want to think about sex with her sitting three feet away in a chair steadily working on her laptop, ignoring him. No, that wasn't true. He simply wanted her thinking about sex as well. This was yet one more opportunity.

He read the first question. Which of the following most closely expresses your views on oral sex? A) I'm only into receiving. B) It's better to give than receive. C) 69, gets us both there in half the time. What the heck? He scanned farther down.

List your five favorite positions in descending order, number one being your favorite. Huh?

Name your top five fantasies in descending order.

Startled, he looked across at Abby. She wanted to know *this*? She glanced up from her computer screen. "Are you through?"

"Uh, no."

"Is there a problem?"

"Uh, kind of."

A slight frown censored him. "I really can't help you with any of it, because they're supposed to be unprompted answers."

"I wasn't expecting…well, this…uh…depth of questioning."

"Really? There's nothing special in there that I recall. But I suppose it's very telling that you're uncomfortable with some of it, I'll make a note of it. Just do the best you can, okay? Think of it as a standardized test with no right or wrong answers. It will just tell me a little bit more about you."

Sure. It was practically a freaking SAT of sexuality. Okay. And he was supposed to list his top five fantasies, just spell them out on paper for her to read? No way.

He glanced back at the sex survey and drew in a deep

breath. Wasn't this what he wanted, her thinking of him in conjunction with sex? If she could ask this kind of stuff without blinking an eye, he'd answer it. He only hoped she was ready to discover the real Deke.

CHAPTER SIX

"I'M THROUGH."

Abby glanced up from the same screen she'd been staring at for the last five minutes without making much headway. She hadn't added much to the document she was working on, but she had come up with a contingency plan. None of this sexual attraction humming between her and Deke was real. It was simply a matter of proximity and subject matter. As long as Deke remembered his dream girl and she remembered she was nothing more than a project manager, all should be fine and they'd have a real success on their hands.

Deke stood and rolled his neck, as if sore from holding that position too long. Actually, Abby was surprised at how long it had taken him to run through what was a fairly straightforward questionnaire, especially since there was no right or wrong answer, it was all preference.

She put aside her laptop and stood as well. She reached for the sheaf of papers. "Great. I'll give this a read-through and then we'll move on."

Deke handed them to her and took a step back,

bumping into the couch. Now that she knew what an incredible kisser he was, well, his geeky fumbling didn't seem nearly so geeky. "I think I'll just take the dogs for a walk if you think Minerva will go with me."

"She loves walks. You'll have a friend for life but you'll have to watch her with other dogs. Actually, she's so little that you'll really have to watch her with people on the sidewalk too. Maybe I should take her after I look this over."

Deke smiled, his eyes crinkling at the corners. "I promise I'll take good care of your baby. That is, if you can trust me to look after her."

He wasn't being flippant or sarcastic. She knew he understood how much Mini meant to her because she sensed Mac was equally important to him.

He trusted her to turn his life around, surely she could trust him with something important to her as well.

"Thank you. I know you'll take care of her."

His eyes held hers. "I will."

He retrieved the leashes and called both dogs. Mac and Mini, the original odd couple, promptly trotted in. Mac stood patiently while Deke hooked the leash to his collar while Mini executed her usual happy dance on her hind legs. Deke laughed as he leashed Minerva. He glanced at Abby over his shoulder, "Do I need to carry her down the stairs?"

Not only was he great with animals, he was thoughtful as well. "That's sweet of you to offer. It'd definitely be easier on her knees."

"No problem. Can I get you something to drink before I leave? Tea? Coffee? Water?"

Maybe a stiff shot of Scotch to burn off the lingering heat of that kiss and the image of him nearly naked? "No thanks. I'm fine. When you get back we'll see a stylist, grab some lunch and do some shopping. It won't take me that long to go through this. Would you mind if I took a look through your closet while you're gone or would you prefer for me to wait until you're back? It would help to know if any of your wardrobe is salvageable before we buy anything else."

"Look through anything you want to while I'm gone. I certainly don't have any secrets anymore." He picked up Minerva who seemed perfectly content to be held against his side. Smart dog. Deke had a very nice side, as Abby had learned first-hand not too long ago. "Which brings up another point. You know so much about me— or at least, you will." He glanced toward the questionnaire. "I only know you from work. It's a little awkward baring your soul to someone who's a virtual stranger. I think you should fill out a questionnaire too so that I'll know you a bit more."

Abby pursed her lips, considering his request. It was reasonable enough. The questions were fairly innocuous and it stood to reason he'd be more relaxed if he knew more about her. And actually, aside from his initial plea for help, he'd demanded nothing else from her. She knew clients always had demands, so to comply with this one seemed easy enough. "Sure. I can do that. No problem."

"And you won't skip any of the sections? You wouldn't ask me to tell you anything you wouldn't tell me in return?"

"Of course not." Wasn't that the sign of a good manager? She wouldn't ask anyone working on a project to do something she wouldn't. Well, maybe not, because she really wasn't willing to strip down to her underwear for him but thank God he hadn't asked. Although, heaven help her if he kissed her first and requested afterwards. Actually, she was ridiculously flattered that he was interested in the details of her life. "I'll make sure I fill out the whole thing."

His smile nearly stole her breath. "Okay. We'll be back soon."

Abby watched as Deke left with the dogs. He really was a very nice guy and now that she knew what lay beneath the T-shirt that hung too big and the shapeless jeans, well…. The more she discovered about him, the more Deke Foster intrigued her. And she had a feeling she'd only scratched his surface.

She picked up the questionnaire but tossed it back on the coffee table. She stood, driven by a restless energy. She might as well check out his closet before she read through the paperwork. Besides, she wouldn't mind stretching her legs a bit.

Deke hadn't actually taken her into his bedroom earlier, but merely pointed in that direction. She opened the door and stepped inside. It felt oddly intimate to be in here now. She pushed the thought away and crossed the room, doing her best to ignore the sensual pull of the four-poster bed with the chocolate duvet cover.

She stopped in the middle of the room and ran her hand along the headboard. Sensual pull? For goodness sake, it was just another bed. There was no reason for her to be experiencing the crazy tingly warmth that radiated through her. Except she'd seen him stripped down, and now she was superimposing that image on the bed in front of her—Deke, naked, with sheets tangled around his legs and waist, his dark eyes hungry, his body stretched above her, pressing her down into that mattress while his talented mouth roved over her.... Her nipples tightened and in the amount of time it took for the image to flash through her brain, she grew wet and hot. She shook her head. She wasn't frigid by any stretch of the imagination, but she also didn't usually find herself fantasizing to the point of arousal after one hot kiss. Maybe Margo was right and Deke was priming her pump, so to speak.

She marched over to his closet. Jeans and slacks were hung together. Shirts and T-shirts in another section. It was neat and organized and...hideous. Whereas all the furnishings in the house proclaimed understated male elegance, his closet was a visual assault of color and patterns. She wasn't surprised, because she'd seen how atrociously he dressed at work, but why? What had he said to her earlier? He was glad she hadn't found his home boring. Was that it? Was this some misguided attempt at being hip because if he showed the world what he really liked, they'd find him boring? Or maybe it was some kind of weird reverse psychology. If he resembled a mad scientist with his bad haircut, bushy beard and wild clothes, then maybe he'd just be dismissed as eccentric and no one would ever try to find the real Deke Foster. And therefore no one would find him lacking. Heck, she didn't know because she didn't have a psychology degree, but she did know all of these clothes had to go. Today.

She closed the closet and avoided eye contact with his bed. It evoked something deep and sexual inside her and she didn't need to go there right now. She still had to read through his questionnaire and then fill out the other one before he returned with the dogs.

She'd been on the sofa earlier but now she kicked off her shoes and settled herself in the butter-soft leather armchair, tucking her feet beneath her. This was obviously Deke's chair. His scent clung to the leather. She began to read through the questionnaire. His favorite color was brown—not a surprise now that she'd seen his house, but it could have been a little misleading if she hadn't known he'd done the browns in a very elegant masculine way. He held a masters degree in information technology from MIT—that explained the sweatshirt. He hailed from Iowa. Two brothers, one older, one younger. His views on oral sex were…. What? Where had that come from? She scanned the rest of the page… and the one after that…and the one after that!

She threw the papers down and jumped out of the

chair. Embarrassment scorched her and a different type of heat radiated from between her thighs. There was nothing geeky or boring about his fantasies. They were quite…arousing.

She paced from the marble fronted fireplace across to the far wall and back. What had he said? The depth of questioning? And she'd told him it was nothing special?

Margo. This had Margo written all over it—Margo who was in danger of dying or suffering a serious injury when Abby got her hands on her. Last night after she'd colored Margo's hair, they'd finished that pitcher of margaritas and Abby had forgotten all about the questionnaire until this morning. Obviously Margo had decided to *spice up* Abby's questions.

Abby could hardly tell Deke her neighbor had decided to insert a little ad lib section. She'd be caught talking about him as a project, which was the height of unprofessionalism. She could always say she'd mixed up some paperwork but that would leave him wondering why she'd had *that* type of paperwork in the first place. Her third option, the one she felt she had no choice but to run with, was to say nothing.

And then there was the little matter of her having to fill out her own questionnaire. What was it he'd said? Don't skip any sections. He'd tricked her. Manipulated her. No, that wasn't true. Margo had played the trick. He hadn't known she had no idea those sexual questions were in there. And she'd been so cavalier when he'd stumblingly brought it up…oh, God. But he'd had the guts to fill it out…in what appeared to be quite honest detail. And she'd promised.

So she picked up a pen…and began filling in her answers.

CHAPTER SEVEN

"Ohhh. *Trés magnifique*. It is like silk, *non?*" Celeste, Abby's hair stylist for the last four years, appeared on the verge of imminent orgasm as she winnowed her hands through Deke's hair. "Ab-bee, you must feel his hair. It is wonderful."

Deke, who'd blushed like the last adult male virgin in D.C. when he'd bumped into her earlier sat there getting the mother of all scalp massages, smirking.

Celeste beckoned her, "Come. Run your fingers through his magnifique hair."

Hair was hair but if Celeste was about to have a public moment and wanted Abby to participate, who was she to play the spoilsport? Abby walked over and lifted her hands to his hair. Celeste was right. It flowed against her skin like burnished silk.

Maybe it was her hairdresser's Gallic exaggeration, but some imp overtook her as she buried her fingers against his scalp, offering her own near-orgasmic performance. "Yes, he is truly *magnifique,* Celeste."

Two of the other patrons and their stylist all laughed. As she pulled her hands out of his hair, Deke captured her wrist, encircling it with his fingers. Slowly, almost lazily, he drew it to his mouth.

"Save it…for later," he murmured, his breath a warm rush against her skin. He pressed a brief kiss to her now-frantic pulse and his lips set fire to her flesh, causing a storm of heat and longing to sweep through her. He released her and she could only stand and stare at him, feeling decidedly light-headed. God in heaven, it was the craziest thing, but she felt seduced by a simple kiss to her wrist. Deke was doing exactly what she'd instructed him to do. He was practicing…and for a geeky guy with a still-bad haircut, he was amazingly good at it.

Celeste uttered a throaty laugh. "Ah. I see, *mon amie*." Her look transcended speculation with its knowing. Small wonder Celeste thought they were more than friends. If she didn't know their arrangement, she might think the same thing. "Celeste knows just what to do with your *friend's* hair."

"Not too short," she rasped. Was that really her voice?

"Ah, it was meant for a woman to run her fingers through, *non?*"

"No. I mean yes."

Once again, Celeste laughed and snapped her fingers at the wash station attendant. "Come, take him back and ready him for me." She turned to Deke. "And you, *cheri,* must give your glasses to Ab-bee. She will hold them for you. They will only be in the way for what we are about to do, *non?*"

Honestly, did Celeste have to make it sound as if

they were about to go at it with one another? Deke handed her his glasses. His fingers brushed against hers and again heat exploded in her, through her. Celeste waved her hands at Abby, shooing her away. "Wait out front. I will bring him to you when he's ready."

Abby went to the front as Celeste had ordered and settled into a plump-cushioned chair. She thought about phoning Margo on her cell phone while she waited but she realized she was too nervous.

She picked up a magazine off the top of the stack without looking at it. It took all of her willpower not to rush to the back and demand Celeste do nothing. She didn't want to change him. She'd developed a serious case of lust for Deke Foster just the way he was, with his shaggy hair, wild beard and ill-fitting clothes.

But this wasn't about her. This was about Deke and the job she'd agreed to do for him.

Celeste was a genius with a pair of scissors. She cost a fortune but talent didn't come cheap and Celeste intuitively knew the best cut to flatter. If she announced she was moving to Timbuktu, Abby would willingly fly there once a month. A bad hair day wasn't in Celeste's artistic vocabulary.

Abby tossed the magazine back on the stack, uninterested in reading. Now and then Celeste's accented English and Deke's deeper, lower voice punctuated the noise of numerous conversations, blow dryers, and the telephone. The minutes seemed to drag until finally Celeste's heels sounded across the floor.

"*Voilá. Il est beau, n'est-ce pas?* He is a handsome man is he not, your friend?"

Abby stood and looked beyond Celeste to Deke and her heart hammered against her ribs. She should've followed her instincts and stopped Celeste while she could.

"Well, say something," Celeste demanded.

"Wonderful. You've done a wonderful job."

Hair that had once looked shaggy and unkempt still brushed Deke's collar, but it now fell in brown gleaming waves that drew attention to his dark eyes with their thick brown lashes. Celeste had shaved his jaws clean, revealing a strong jaw and cheekbones. She'd trimmed his mustache and the rest of his beard to a neat, tidy goatee that gave him a swashbuckling look and showcased a well-shaped mouth.

This was far, far worse than she'd anticipated. Deke Foster was devastatingly sexy.

DEKE PUSHED HIS GLASSES UP, no easy feat considering all of the shopping bags he carried, as they climbed the steps to the third floor. Abby had her hands full as well.

"Thank you, Abby."

"You're welcome, Deke. Just doing my job."

Which he might've believed if he hadn't seen the flash of jealousy in her silver eyes when Celeste had run her fingers through his hair. He'd felt like shouting for joy. He hadn't imagined the connection that ran between them. She felt it too. And that brief glimpse of possessiveness had occurred before his hair cut and beard trim. Before the new clothes. Before his new look.

He unlocked the door and stepped back for her to enter first. He followed her in and they both headed to his bedroom to drop off the shopping bags containing his new wardrobe. "I should've got another dog a long time ago. Usually Mac meets me at the door and knocks me down. Or at least, he tries to…"

"Mini probably wore him out."

He followed her down the hall to his bedroom. Before they'd left for the afternoon, he'd read through her questionnaire. All of it. Her fantasy list was seared in his brain. Now, all he could think of was the fantasy that had made both their lists. The shared fantasy of a four-poster bed and silk scarves.

Abby all but threw his packages on the bed and then backed away. Hmm, that fantasy was obviously front and center in her mind as well. Heat and awareness lurked in her eyes.

"So…" She looked at him from the end of his bed.

He imagined her, sprawled naked…wrists and ankles bound to each post…her eyes hot…expose…ready…

"So…" He didn't know what to say.

In his fantasy, he moved over her and kissed the arch of her foot, laved the delicate turn of her ankle with his tongue. He moved slowly, intent on kissing, tasting every inch of her before burying himself between her open, awaiting thighs…

Or maybe he'd be bound to the bed while she tortured

him with the exquisite drag of her lips and tongue against his bare flesh…

Abby looked away from Deke and wet her lips with the tip of her tongue. She knew.

She cleared her throat as if that could dispel the fantasy that pulsed between them. "I'm really pleased with the way today has gone." She nodded. "We've accomplished a tremendous amount. That's good considering we only have a short amount of time to get you ready for…what is your lady's name? You've never said."

He ached to tell her the truth, but it was too soon. He was battling more than his geekiness. Abby kept her heart as closely guarded as Fort Knox. "Cara. Her name is Cara." Not quite the truth but close enough. Cara meant "dear one" in Italian, one of the most beautiful languages in the world, and Abby had had his heart from day one. "You think Cara will be pleased?"

Her smile didn't quite reach her eyes. She'd asked him to put a name to his woman, but she wasn't as immune as she'd have him believe. "Cara would have to be unconscious not to be pleased." She walked out of his bedroom and back toward the den. Panic swamped him as he followed her through the hall. She couldn't be ready to wrap up his make-over yet.

"I still don't think I'm ready," he blurted, his voice holding a note of desperation.

She began packing up her papers and laptop. She paused to look up at him. "You're not."

He wasn't sure if he was disappointed that she still found him lacking or relieved, because it meant he'd have more time with her.

"So, what's the next step?"

She slid her laptop into her padded briefcase. "We've taken care of the window dressing. Now you've got to practice interacting."

"With you, right? So I'm ready for Cara."

"Yes. Remember, I'm your beta. We need to practice going out, socially."

"So I'll practice dating with you." The concept was geeky, he knew, but he liked it. "What would you like to do tomorrow, Abby? Pick something you'd really enjoy doing on a date." *Please, don't let it be salsa dancing or something equally above his two left-footed capabilities. Although if she wanted to salsa, he'd salsa.* "What's your idea of a perfect date?" He already knew with arousing, tempting certainty what her top five ideas for perfect sex were.

"A picnic in the park." She answered so quickly, so unhesitatingly that he knew she'd been honest. "And maybe we could take the dogs along. If you don't think that's too boring."

"It sounds perfect. Is there a park near your place? If not, Franklin's within easy walking distance of here." He grinned in relief. "I was afraid you'd want to go salsa dancing or something," he admitted.

She laughed and her eyes sparkled. "No. Not this girl. I'm not a big dancer. I prefer listening to music than dancing to it. So, salsa dancing's out and the park's in unless there's something else you'd rather do."

They could always take turns working their way through their lists... "The park sounds great. We can stop by Hanson's deli on the way and pick up lunch."

Minerva pranced in, her toenails clicking on the hardwood floor, and began to dance around. Abby clipped on the little dog's leash. Mac lumbered into the room behind her, wearing a mournful expression.

Deke offered a rueful smile. "I don't think he's ready for her to go." He knew he wasn't ready for Abby to leave. "We'll walk you to your car." He grabbed the leash from its hook beside the door.

"That's not necessary," Abby protested.

"No, it's not, is it?" Deke snapped the leash into place on Mac's collar. "But we'll do it anyway."

He and Mac escorted Abby and Minerva downstairs and halfway down the block to her car. Even with spring hovering around the corner, night had fallen in the space of time since they'd gotten in from shopping.

Light pooled from streetlamps along the sidewalk and they stopped half a dozen times along the way for both dogs to sniff and christen every corner post and tree between Deke's house and Abby's car. The slight breeze that wrapped Abby's scent around him also slid over his face and reminded him of his cleanly shaved jaw. He supposed he looked different, a new package, but he still felt the same inside.

"We'll be going now." Abby opened the passenger

door and placed Minerva in the front seat. She closed the door and turned to face him. "We'll see you tomorrow a little before noon then?"

"Sure. It's a date." He shifted from one foot to the other.

She looked up at him, her eyes almost colorless in the glow from the streetlight. She reached up and pressed a quick kiss to his lips. "Goodnight, Deke."

He stood rooted to the sidewalk, not quite believing that she'd just kissed him, while she got in her car and pulled away from the curb.

"Goodnight, *cara mia,*" he murmured as her taillights faded from sight. What would she say when she found out she was his cara?

CHAPTER EIGHT

"I THINK IT MUST BE LOVE," Abby said the next afternoon as she sat on the blanket, her arms wrapped around her knees. Mac and Mini, worn out from the walk to the park and a game of fetch with Deke, lay curled together, half on the blanket, half in the green grass.

The sun had begun to edge its way toward the horizon and still she was loath to call an end to a day that had been so perfect. Deke was incredibly easy to talk to. They'd talked about his childhood, growing up on an Iowa farm and Abby's growing up in suburbia, locked in the mortal combat of her parents' divorce—which, incidentally she'd never before discussed without alcohol or coercion. This time both had been conspicuously missing.

They'd traded jokes, some corny, some clean, some dirty, but all hilariously funny. They'd talked about movies and music and the state of world affairs. She'd told him about her cat Pip, the one who'd seen her through the dark days of her parents' divorce and who'd died the year she married Lyle. He confided in her about his college roommate Greg and how he had been more of a brother than a friend, and tried to make her understand the gaping hole his death had left in Deke's life.

In one afternoon, she'd divulged more to Deke than she had to Lyle during the entire span of the marriage. Of course, the difference was that Deke had *wanted* to know. And underlying all their conversation had been a current of awareness that had lent a supercharged nuance to every look, touch, laugh. She'd spent an afternoon connected to Deke Foster in a way she'd never been connected to another human being. Abby wasn't sure whether she found it heady or frightening. But even the dogs seemed to be tuned in.

Deke lay on his side, propped on one elbow, slightly behind her. He laughed and pulled her back and down until his chest pillowed her shoulders and head. His heartbeat thudded beneath her ear and she was intensely aware of his scent and his heat.

Lying against him was intimate and comfortable and unsettling all combined. They'd discussed the rules this morning. They'd spend the day together as if they were a real couple on a real date. Abby didn't think it'd help Deke's self-consciousness or his self-confidence if she constantly reminded him they were role playing. Even if she had to keep silently reminding herself.

"I think Mac's definitely smitten." His laugh rumbled against her shoulders. "Crazy as it sounds, he was pining until Mini got back today."

"She could barely sit still in the car. I think she was hoping we were coming back to see you."

He tucked a curl behind her ear and his touch fueled an internal heat. "What do you suppose she sees in him? He's big and sort of goofy."

"Well, obviously she sees beyond that." She snared his fingers in her own. "He shares his toys with her and he obviously adores her. What's not to love there?"

"Is that the key to women? Sharing my toys and unstinting devotion?" He twined his fingers in hers.

"It doesn't hurt."

"And what's the key to Abby Vandiver? What kind of man do you want?" His mouth smiled but his eyes were piercing, serious.

One like you. The thought flashed through her mind like a jolt of lightning in a summer heat storm, blinding, illuminating. And it wasn't just because of the haircut and the new clothes. She'd felt an attraction to him long before then. Heck maybe from the moment she'd noticed his eyes in her office. And though she knew he was doing all of this for a woman named Cara, she also knew the attraction wasn't one-sided.

"What kind of man do I want? I think it's someone who is a combination of sexy, smart and successful, with a sense of humor, someone who won't try to stifle me to feed his ego. And if he treated me with a healthy dose of unstinting devotion, it would go a long way as well."

"And how would you like your man packaged?"

"This will probably sound very odd coming from

me, but it doesn't really matter as long as he's comfortable in his own skin."

He smiled, causing the corner of his eyes to crinkle, sending her pulse dancing. "I'm still a geek aren't I?" His chocolate brown eyes were rueful, not dismayed.

"Yes. You are." There was nothing wrong with a little light flirtation, she assured herself. It was good for him. "But you're a really, really sexy geek."

He shoved at his glasses and a wave of red washed over his neck and up his face. "You don't have to say that…you know…because…"

Had he been any other man, she might've suspected blatant manipulation. But despite the physical changes, Deke still didn't get it. "You really don't have any idea do you?"

She shifted onto her side until she faced him, her body perpendicular to his on the blanket. "I'm not going to be anything other than honest with you because it doesn't do you any good otherwise. So, you have to take me at my word. You're gorgeous. Your hair is silky and sexy with it being a little longer like that. And you have incredible eyes."

"Incredible?" He looked away from her. "I think you're making fun of me—"

"Fun of you? Surely you know you have beautiful eyes." Apparently he didn't, so it was up to her to set the record straight. "They're like pools of rich dark chocolate. With just the right look from those eyes you could a melt a woman from the inside out."

"I think you need to teach me that look." His eyes held hers and it felt like a private lesson.

"Okay. Here's an important distinguishing point. Look at me as if you wonder what it would be like to kiss me. Do not look at me as if you wonder what I look like naked. Women don't want to be visually stripped— well, not at first maybe. And you don't want to peer too hard at her mouth or she'll think she's got a piece of broccoli wedged in her teeth."

"Like this?" He looked at her mouth as if he'd like to kiss her until she felt like she'd weep with pleasure or need or both. And she did, indeed, feel as if she was melting from the inside out.

"Yes. Exactly like that."

"Really?" He did it again.

Heat pooled low in her belly and slicked her thighs. "Yes. Really."

"Are you melting from the inside out?"

"I'm close to puddling at your feet." She'd thought to lighten things up with a joke, but it came out…different. Breathy. Wanting. "You can stop now. I think you've got it down pat."

"Okay. I'll practice later." His slow smile simmered through her.

God, she was practically handing him a loaded gun. But it was crucial to the project's success and she always saw a project through to a successful end.

Ruthlessly, she continued. "You have a very sensual mouth." She angled her head to one side and studied his mouth. "Perfect really. Your lips aren't too full but they're not too thin either. Women will look at your mouth and they'll think its eminently kissable."

He flushed. "You've got to be kidding."

"Do I look as if I'm kidding? And I'm not trying to embarrass you. These are your assets. You need to be aware of them. Not to abuse them. Not to be arrogant, but to know what you have, because this is you, it's what you are. You need to know that you have a classic bone structure that's pleasing in a man. High cheekbones, sculpted jaw, a nose that would make Michelangelo's David envious. Twenty, thirty, even forty years from now, you'll still be a handsome man because you have excellent bone structure."

She'd read a bit and it was important for him to think of himself in sexual, sensual terms because people projected their own self-awareness onto others. Still, she couldn't help feeling that she'd somehow crossed a line. That she'd gone from self-empowering to seduction. But she seemed patently unable to stop herself. She was caught up in a riptide of attraction. She knew from childhood summers spent at the beach that you could drown trying to fight a riptide. The secret was to relax and let it carry you out to sea…then you swam back to shore.

"You have a body that leaves women weak at the knees, or at least it will, now that you're wearing clothes that fit and a woman can actually see your broad shoulders and trim waist."

She took his hand in hers. "Look at your hands. Beautiful. A woman will look at your hands and know they're instruments of pleasure. She'll imagine them touching her, stroking her, sliding across her skin, your fingers tangling in her hair, feathering across her face…"

"Abby…"

"You need to know that your voice is very sexy too. You could be talking about the weather, but your voice sends a tingle down a woman's spine and a trail of heat through her body, like a shot of fine, aged whiskey." He leaned forward, his mouth mere inches from hers.

Her breath caught in her throat and it occurred to her that she was in real danger of seducing herself on his behalf. "But the absolute sexiest thing about you is that you're an intelligent, thoughtful, interesting man who has more layers than a woman could ever discover in a lifetime."

His lips feathered along her jaw, more of a caress than a kiss. "Do *you* think that when you look at me? Is that what you feel?"

She couldn't deny it. Didn't want to deny it. She knew where this was going and she wanted to ride the dangerous current to the sea. Tomorrow, she'd swim to safety. She leaned into his warmth, her lips finding his jaw. "Yes."

He pulled her to her feet and into the warm, hard line of his body. "Let's go home."

CHAPTER NINE

THE DOOR CLOSED BEHIND HIM and Deke, after unleashing both dogs, didn't bother to turn on the light. Instead he did what he'd longed to do all the way back from the park—he took her in his arms. But he needed to go slow. He started by feathering his fingers along the fine skin of her jaw, that simple touch of her face unleashing a torrent of want and heat within him. If she'd spoken the truth earlier, it affected her the same.

He cupped her jaw in his hand and dipped his head to scatter kisses along her jaw to her neck to the curve of her shoulder. Her faint tremor shuddered through him as well. Passion was all the sweeter, and hotter, when it was shared.

"Don't go, Abby. Stay with me tonight. All night," he murmured against the tender column of her neck.

A part of him wanted to challenge her to stay because she wanted to, not because it was some conditioning or training. But he didn't have the guts. He wanted her regardless of the terms. Nor did he want her to think too hard because he didn't want her walking out the door. He wrapped his hand around the curve of her neck. "I want you in my bed tonight."

He swooped down, crushing her mouth beneath his and still she buried her hands in his hair, tugging him closer. Her mouth, hot and eager, demanded as much as it offered. Her pillowy soft lips rained fierce hungry kisses against his mouth.

"Stay," he beseeched.

"Yes," she acquiesced.

He couldn't recall if it had been number one or two on her fantasy list but he remembered one of those fantasies vividly—*against the door, in the dark, like the closet scene from page twenty-seven of Puzo's The Godfather.*

"It's not a closet, but it's nearly dark." The kitchen light was only a faint glow in the next room. "And it's a door…" he murmured suggestively against her mouth.

"Yes," she breathed. Her fingers dug into his shoulders. "Now."

Her command wasn't a problem. He'd wanted her since he'd first seen her. And who knew how long she'd carried this fantasy in her head? He only knew he planned to deliver on it—now.

He skimmed his hands down her sides to the waist of her jeans. For a split second the button stuck, but then it gave way. He unzipped her pants and tugged them down her hips while his mouth locked on to hers, his tongue thrusting against hers.

She ran her hands over his shoulders and down his chest. She slid one hand to the front of his jeans and cupped him. Even through the layer of denim and boxer cotton, her touch scorched him and damn near sent him over the edge, especially when she moaned into his mouth. Or was that his moan? He didn't know. His heart raced, keeping pace with his throbbing erection. He pulled his mouth from hers, his breath ragged, needy. She panted against him.

"I don't want to go too fast," he said. "Are you ready?"

"Yes." She uttered the single syllable in a tight, husky gasp while she toed off her shoes and wiggled out of her jeans. He dug in his wallet for a condom—finally, after years of carrying one in readiness, he needed one. Well, it wasn't exactly the same one but.... She reached between them and yanked his zipper down.

He hadn't read page twenty-seven but it struck him as likely that sex in a dark closet up against the door wasn't tender and slow, but hot, hungry and frantic, which pretty much summed up his mental and physical state. Abby reached inside his boxers and whatever thought process he'd once laid claim to died in his brain when she wrapped her hand around the length of his cock and made an appreciative noise, half moan, half murmur in the back of her throat.

Abby released him long enough for him to roll on his condom. Then he drove her back against the door. She offered a sharp, approving gasp as his mouth captured hers and his erection nudged between her thighs. She rocked her hips against him, damn near sending him over the edge.

His Abby. His woman. He reached between her thighs. Wet panties. One good rip and they were gone, tossed to the floor. She writhed against him and moaned into his mouth. He tested his finger against her slick swollen cleft and she dug her nails into his shoulders and spread her legs.

Deke grasped her buttocks in his hands and lifted her off the ground and against the door. She wrapped her legs around him, pulling him closer with her feet against his buttocks. He plunged into her channel.

Tight.

Hot.

Wet.

Her muscles clenched around him and she moaned into his mouth, her pleasure vibrating against his tongue. In and out. Harder. Faster. Until she clenched her muscles around him in the beginning notes of an orgasm and he swallowed her cries of release, echoing them back with his own.

It had been hard and fast…and absolutely perfect. Abby had owned his heart from the moment he'd met her. New he'd handed her his soul.

ABBY SLOWLY OPENED her eyes, even though Deke was little more than a dark silhouette. "That was incredible," she said.

Deke lifted his head from where he still had her pinned against his front door. His warm breath swirled deliciously against her neck. "It was, wasn't it?" She sensed his smile and heard the same sexual satisfaction she felt. "I haven't read the book, so I hope I got page twenty-seven right."

She laughed and in a moment of heady aftermath

licked his neck. "You could've written the book." She wasn't tacky enough to tattle, but while she might not say it, she could certainly think it. Lyle had never managed to get that fantasy right. They'd tried twice and then she'd cut him off before he totally ruined it for her.

"You're a good instructor." Ohhh. His voice, all husky and rough from good sex, sent a shiver straight through her. She felt him pulse deep inside her in response. Despite the fact that she was still basking in great orgasm afterglow, something stirred again in her.

"I didn't give any instructions," she said, somewhat baffled, yet perfectly content to carry on a conversation with her legs wrapped around his waist and his cock buried in her up to the hilt. She'd never met a man as tuned into her as Deke was.

"Hmm. But you did. You gave plenty of non-verbal instruction that shouted what you wanted."

"Really? Like what?"

"Like when you touched me through my jeans."

"Very perceptive." She laughed softly. "That was definitely something I wanted quite desperately."

"And then there was the way you moaned into my mouth when you liked something. It was quite a turn-on."

Damn, if he wasn't sending tremors of want through her again. And…wow…sweet mercy, he must be feeling the same because he was beginning to harden inside her again.

"You're a good listener," she said, clenching her muscles around his quickly recovering cock.

With his weight holding her up, he skimmed his hands beneath her sweater to her breasts. She sucked in a deep breath when he rolled her nipples between his fingers. "You're an eloquent speaker," he countered.

He tugged her bra beneath her breasts, leaving them open to his cleverly marauding fingers. Abby bit her lip, aching for his mouth to replace his hands. "You're very good with instructions yourself," she said, her breath quickening.

His low laugh whispered through her, wickedly suggestive. "You think? What am I saying now?"

"You're saying you'd like for us both to get naked in your bed."

He tugged her sweater up and flicked his tongue against one tight, aching bud. "That's a start…"

Oh. He'd captured the other one and bit down with just the right amount of pressure, sizzling the most delightful sensation through her whole body.

"And then there's this fantasy list we need to discuss," she said.

"An all-night discussion? I'm up for it if you are."

"Promises. Promises."

CHAPTER TEN

ABBY AWOKE COCOONED in the warmth of Deke's arms—safe, sated, happy.

She blinked her eyes open, panic and fear crowding in on her. She had no business feeling those things—all those buzz words that lulled you, left you vulnerable and then left a gaping wound when they went away.

She didn't regret last night. It had been…beyond compare. But she wasn't about to get off track and misstep this morning.

It was time for her to swim back to shore. She had enough sense to know if she stayed in warm deep water, she'd eventually drown in something that was much more dangerous than mere sex.

DEKE ROLLED OVER and reached for Abby, his eyes still closed, only to encounter the same emptiness that greeted him every other morning. What the…? He swung out of bed and didn't bother with his jeans or boxers. It wasn't as if she hadn't seen him naked last night. A nasty foreboding gnawed at his gut because last night had been altogether far too perfect.

"Abby," he yelled her name. "Abby? Mini?"

This morning was the time to come clean. To tell her *she* was his Cara. To confess he'd been in love with her since the first time he'd seen her. And he'd planned to tell her in bed—except she wasn't in his bed.

He made it as far as the den when Abby rounded the corner coming out of his office—fully clothed to his dismay. Except he knew she was pantyless beneath those jeans.

Gone was the woman who'd dragged her talented tongue over his body in arousing detail in the early hours of the morning. Instead, he met Abby Vandiver, the polished professional. "Good morning. I tried to be quiet. I took the dogs out for a quick walk before I showered. Mini and I will be out of here in a few minutes."

"Out of here?" He sounded like an idiot but what the hell was she talking about? "I don't want you out of here. I want you back in my bed."

Her eyes that had seemed like molten steel last night in the throws of passion, were now cool mirrors that revealed nothing. "That's not going to happen."

"I didn't notice any complaints last night."

"Don't be obtuse. Of course there weren't any. You were better than good…which tells me you're ready. I've done my job."

Talk about a "what-the-hell" moment. "What?"

"You're ready," she repeated. "For Cara."

He'd loved her with every fiber of his being last night, and she still didn't know? "After last night you're willing to turn me over to another woman?" He laughed because he didn't know what else to do. "You're kidding right?"

She arched one cool brow in his direction. "Let me remind you that *she's* what this whole repackaging was all about."

Didn't last night count for *anything?* He'd felt connected, whole, for the first time in his life and he'd be damned if she hadn't felt it as well. "I love you, Abby."

"No you don't. There's a name for this and it's quite common. I've transformed you and you're so pleased with the new you that you've transferred your affections to me. You're not in love with me. Not really. And you're better off realizing it now and chalking it up to a night of good sex."

Her eyes were cool. He was locked out. He knew then that nothing he said would make a difference but he had to try one last time. "It was more than that and you know it."

"What? Please. Don't make this out to be something it's not."

"There's a connection between us."

"Sure, physically you do it for me. And you're a nice enough guy—except for the fact that you slept with me when you profess to love another woman." She looked at him as if he were something a careless dog owner had left littering the sidewalk. "I don't need that kind of man, Deke. But I assure you Cara will never hear about this from me." She called Mini.

"So, last night meant nothing and you're willing to turn me over to Cara just like that?"

She shrugged. "I told you. It was good. You were good." She picked up the little dog who'd obediently but reluctantly appeared.

Abby could've carved his heart out and left it on the kitchen counter and it would've hurt less. Wounded, he fired back. "How much extra do I owe you for last night? Or do you just want to tack it on to my fee?"

A brief flicker in her eyes told him he'd scored a direct hit. Instead of triumph though, he just felt more miserable. She snapped on Mini's leash and opened the front door. "Consider it a freebie," she said as she walked out. "A bonus at no extra charge."

"WELL, HERE WE ARE. Just the two of us. At least I know who I can count on," Abby said to Mini as they crawled through the miserable miasma known as Monday morning rush hour in D.C. At least they didn't have to tackle the beltway. And now she didn't even have the distraction of work since she'd insisted they each take three days off. But then again, she'd have never guessed that Deke would have transformed himself in such a short period. That was okay. She'd make use of her time and after that her next project from home until she went back to the office. And then she'd work on the project after that and the one after that. And that would be her life…a succession of one project after another to try and plug all the empty holes.

Damn Deke Foster to geek hell for showing her what

her life was missing. For dangling what could be before her. She'd walked away from Lyle and three years of marriage without any remorse. Why did she feel now as if she was being ripped apart? Because she'd never loved Lyle the way she loved Deke. The thought stunned her. It was a good thing that traffic sat gridlocked or she might've caused an accident.

How had this happened? She'd never intended to feel anything. She wouldn't allow it. She wanted to put it behind her, but she was stuck here with nowhere to go and nothing to do but face the truth.

He'd told her he loved her and she'd thrown it back in his face. Because, for all her self-assured banter with her girlfriends, she was scared. Scared to let any man in. Scared to take a chance. She'd woken early this morning and the connection she felt to Deke, the way he seemed to tune in to the nuances that were her…the very things that had seemed heady and romantic last night… scared her witless in the harsh light of day.

She'd seen her father destroy her mother by leaving her for another woman. And while Lyle was a jerk, Abby had cheerfully contributed to the demise of her marriage. She'd kept herself safe and inaccessible, even to her husband. She'd made his ego her scapegoat, never attempting to compromise or work things out. And then she'd worn her success and her dedication to her career with pride, flaunted it. She'd never worn it for what it was, a coat of armor that kept her safe from being hurt the way her mother had been.

And now she'd hurt Deke. She'd seen it in his eyes when she'd coolly tossed his love back at him after grinding it beneath her sanctimonious heel. After she'd set him up. And if she was ever going to look at the not so pretty picture that was Abby Vandiver, she had to admit it—she had set the poor guy up to fail. If he slept with her while he was interested in another woman, then it gave her a reason to take what she wanted and walk away afterwards. Neat and tidy and just marginally uncomfortable. Except she knew in her heart that Deke would never sleep with her if he cared about someone else. She knew enough about him now to know that for a fact.

Mini eyed her from the passenger seat and Abby could've sworn reproach glimmered in her eyes. "What? What am I supposed to do? Go crawling back? Tell him I made a mistake? See if they'll still have us? He's not just talking about love here, Mini. If you'll recall he's on the marriage trail. I could drown out there, Min."

Or maybe she'd drown trying to get back to shore, on the same beach she'd been standing on for years. She was heading for the familiar shoreline but maybe it was the wrong one? Maybe Deke was an island she'd overlooked. The new land she'd been afraid to visit?

Mini sniffed delicately and turned to stare out the passenger window at the creeping traffic. Now even Mini was snubbing her.

She supposed she had two choices. Keep heading in

this direction or turn things around. She flicked on her turn signal and crept toward the right hand lane. It was time to choose.

WHY HADN'T HE JUST told her that there was no Cara? That *she* was Cara? Because it wouldn't have made a damn bit of difference. He'd told her he loved her and what had it got him? A metaphorical kick in the balls. She'd been searching for a reason, any reason, to walk out the door. And he was no damn better than she was because he'd let her.

Because she'd turned those wintry gray eyes on him and he'd reverted back to the man who'd spent nearly a year wanting her from a distance but lacking the courage to approach her. And then he'd sought her out to make him over into the man she'd want him to be—only to discover, along the way, that he was already that man on the inside, even before she changed what was on the outside.

If he was going to be the man she wanted, the man she deserved, then he was going to have to stand up for both of them. Fight for what he wanted, even if it meant fighting her. Regardless of what she'd said. Even though she ran away, she cared for him. He'd seen it in her eyes. Felt it in her touch.

No longer was he content to moon around like he'd done for the last year. He knew she'd be stuck in Monday morning rush hour traffic. If he hurried, he could shower and still make it to her place on the Metro before she got there by car. What he'd say when he arrived…well, he wasn't sure. He'd figure it out *on* the way. But he *did* know that she was about to get the truth—whether she wanted it or not.

AS SHE TURNED TO WALK into Deke's building, she and Mini were almost barreled over as he charged down the stairs from the front door to the sidewalk. He grabbed her to steady her on her feet. "Oh. Abby. You're back."

She drew in a deep breath and still felt dizzy, as if she was standing on the edge of a cliff. Mini squirmed impatiently beneath her arm. "I…um…well, I owe you an apology. Do you think we could go back upstairs? Never mind. You were on your way out weren't you?" She was babbling like an idiot and pretty much making a mess of everything.

"I was on my way to your apartment. I thought I'd take the Metro and get there about the same time you did." His brown eyes were cautious, non-committal and she hated that she'd done that to him. "Sure come on up. Mac'll be glad to see Mini."

She preceded him up the stairs in silence. Okay. Mac would be glad to see Mini. But was he glad to see her or was she asking too much after the things she'd said to him such a brief time ago?

Once inside Deke offered to give Mini breakfast, since they hadn't made it home yet. It was as if they were just coming home for the first time in a long time, Abby thought, as Deke measured out kibble for a grateful Mini.

He came back into the room and Abby blurted out the only thing she could, hoping it'd be enough. "I love you, Deke. I was foolish and hateful this morning because I was scared. I hope it's not too little, too late." And then she decided to keep talking because if she did, he couldn't reject her as ruthlessly as she'd rejected him earlier. "Last night was almost magical and it's so scary when someone seems to know you better than you know yourself. People say that's what they want, but when they're actually faced with the prospect, it's downright frightening—"

"Abby." He cut her off mid-babble. "Back up to the first part." The caution in his eyes was giving way to something she was frightened to trust. No, that wasn't true. She wasn't going to be frightened any longer. It was giving way to something she wanted to believe. Desperately.

"The first part?" She stepped close enough to see the hope radiating from his eyes.

"Yeah. Did you just say you loved me?" He pulled her into his arms.

She wrapped her arms around his waist. "I did. Guilty as charged. And I'm so sorry—"

"Shh. The rest doesn't matter. It's just noise. But I have a confession of my own to make."

The bottom dropped out of her stomach, threatening to take her happiness along with it. This had something to do with Cara. She knew it. But instead of following her first instinct to withdraw, she wrapped her arms tighter around him and held on. "Okay."

"There is no Cara. There never has been."

"But, you said… Why make that up?"

"Because I fell in love with you the first time I saw you. I waited almost a year for you to notice me, but after all that time, I was still just Deke the IT geek in your book. After Greg died, well you know the rest of the story… It's all true. But you're Cara."

"I was such an idiot. Such a blind, shortsighted fool." She laughed from sheer happiness. "So, this morning, I essentially accused you of betraying me by sleeping with me."

"Yeah. Something like that."

She pressed a kiss to the underside of his jaw. "Well, I definitely came out on top with this deal. You came to me for a repackage and I'm walking away with the total package."

"And I'd say I came out on top as well."

"How do you figure?" she asked.

He backed her up to the couch, causing her to tumble backward, pulling him down with her.

"Because I know you're not wearing any underwear. And that was number four on my list…"

HER HERO?

Rhonda Nelson

CHAPTER ONE

"THIS IS *SO* NOT HAPPENING."

Flinching as cars zoomed by her along the freeway, Carley DeLuna peered beneath the hood of her brand-new-with-all-the-bells-and-whistles platinum-silver convertible retro Thunderbird and swore repeatedly as steam hissed and popped from the vicinity of the high-tech 280-horsepower, thirty-two-valve DOHC V8 engine.

Ordinarily she wouldn't have known the specs, but she'd carried the little brochure that detailed all the car's features around in her purse for a full six months before ultimately deciding to splurge and make the purchase.

Up until this very moment, she hadn't regretted it.

As a vintage clothing dealer, Carley was visually attracted to older styles. Based in Charlotte, she lived in a 1920s craftsman-style bungalow that had been carefully decorated with aesthetically pleasing bric-a-brac and antiques she'd found at various estate sales and hole-in-the-wall dealers. She loved the smooth, rounded lines of older things, the weight and substance of them, the history and soul stored in things with a past. Carley grimaced.

The trouble was she didn't always love the hit-or-miss reliability that came with them, so the new retro movement of modern conveniences—kitchen appliances and new cars, in particular—had vastly appealed to her. Quite frankly, she could have spent considerably less money on a truly vintage Thunderbird, but it wouldn't have come with the thirty-six-thousand mile bumper-to-bumper warranty. And she'd had enough experience with unreliable clunkers throughout her childhood—on the rare occasions her family had actually *owned* a car—to last her a lifetime.

But this little coupe had been more than merely a way to get herself from Point A to Point B—it was a status symbol, one that proved that she'd arrived, that she'd worked hard and risen above her beginnings in Summertown, North Carolina's public housing complex, the very one her parents had been content to settle for and, disappointingly, still lived in today.

No doubt karma was playing a part in her current circumstances, Carley thought, her conscience pricking her uncomfortably. The truth was her parents' apartment was less than five miles from where she stood and, while she should have exited off the freeway for an obligatory visit, she just couldn't summon the wherewithal to do it.

It was too damned depressing.

The poverty and hopelessness of the area always tightened around her neck, choking her and pulling her away from the hard-won present she could be proud of. It reminded her of meager Christmases and hand-me-down clothes, of hot summers with no air-conditioning and colder winters when heat was a luxury they hadn't been able to afford. But what had really kept her away was the simple fact that she'd never understood her underachieving parents. And they'd never understood their equally overachieving child.

High standards, she thought…both a blessing and a curse.

Had she not driven *past* their exit—irrefutable proof that she hadn't intended to stop—she might have called them to see if her dad could arrange for a tow. The last time she'd talked to her mother, the family car was in the incapable hands of a shade-tree mechanic, so expecting them to be able to offer her a ride was more than she could hope for.

Since their vehicle tended to be parked for repairs more often than it was drivable, her parents had become dependent upon the good will of neighbors and the public transportation system. Carley didn't know how they stood it. Just staring at her crippled car and knowing that it would probably be several days or more before it was repaired was enough to send her into a mild panic.

Furthermore, she didn't have any idea why she'd gotten out of her car and popped the hood to start with. She didn't know what was wrong with it and, even if she could discern an immediate problem—aside from the steam issuing out of the engine—she had no idea how in the hell to fix it. All she'd managed to do was advertise to every would-be rapist or murderer zooming along the freeway that her car had broken down and, as such, she was easy pickings. She grunted at her own stupidity.

As if on cue an old pale blue step-side Chevy pickup pulled in behind her. A dart of panic lodged in her chest and she immediately reached for her cell phone. In all likelihood it was merely a Good Samaritan stopping to help a stranded vehicle—this was the South after all—but a girl could never be too cautious.

Furthermore, Carley thought as she peered around the hood of her car, there was something…oddly familiar about that truck. In fact, she'd lost her virginity in one almost identical to it. A boyish smile, jet-black hair and eyes a watercolor blend of blue and green instantly leapt to mind, bringing back a melancholy mixture of first love and first heartbreak. *Jackson Harper*, Carley thought with a pang of regret. Had her foolish tender heart ever loved a boy more?

Ten years and there was scarcely a day she didn't think about him. She'd often wondered if she'd made a mistake. They'd been childhood friends turned high school sweethearts. He'd slugged a boy on the playground for calling her "poor white trash", then had sheepishly turned to her and asked if she was all right.

Despite everything they would eventually go through together, Carley knew that was the moment she'd ultimately fallen for him. She'd cast him in the role of hero and he'd played the part perfectly…until graduation night, when he'd told her that he was putting college off in favor of working in his father's garage.

Honest work, she knew—and had even known then—but it wasn't the kind of ambition that was ever going to take him out of Summertown, which, unfortunately, she equated with *hell*. Nor wouldn't put him in a much higher tax bracket than her own poor family. Selfish? Shallow? Maybe to some people. But Carley couldn't get past it.

She'd known that an education was the best ticket out of the projects and she'd worked her butt off studying in order to land a scholarship to the University of North Carolina. She'd earned her MBA at Wharton School of Business—where she'd met fellow friends Samantha Stone and Abby Vandiver, who were having equally bad luck in the romance department—and had parlayed her vintage chic boutique into the East coast source for Hollywood's elite.

She'd set high standards for herself and had adhered to them. Was it too much to ask that a guy do the same? It had been too much for Jackson, she remembered now. She'd begged him to reconsider, to give college a chance. She'd counted on her determination and his support to see her through. He'd been her White Knight, her fiercest protector, greatest champion and best friend. With the exception of herself, he'd been the only person in her life that she'd ever expected anything out of…and he'd let her down. Not purposely, of course. But…

"I'm not you, Brownie," he'd said, using the nickname he'd given her in grade school. "I'm content. I don't need what you need."

And he obviously hadn't needed her either, Carley had determined at the time.

Distance had given her a bit of perspective, but there was still a small part of her which clung to the hurt. It was easier than admitting that she'd piled a tall order on his eighteen-year-old shoulders. In retrospect, though, it had all worked out for the best. She'd become the successful businesswoman that she'd always wanted to be, well above the poverty line, and he… Well, she wasn't exactly sure what had become of him. She'd never permitted herself to ask. By now his father had probably retired and he owned the garage himself. And he most likely had a wife who doted upon him and kids who squealed "Daddy!" when he came home at night.

An inexplicable lump formed in her throat.

She blinked, dispelling the vision, only to open her eyes and, to her almost slack-jawed astonishment, saw the mature version of that boy sauntering toward her.

The rangy build of his youth had been replaced with the hard, muscled lines of a man, and the shoulders she'd often rested her head against had widened impossibly over the years. His wavy black hair was a tad longer than he'd worn it way-back-when, but the look suited him. Casually sexy, as though he didn't have much time for frills. He'd paired a navy blue designer T-shirt with worn Levi's and both fabrics hugged a frame that would make any right-thinking woman instantly salivate over what was underneath.

Herself included, Carley thought as her mouth

watered and her heart rate leaped into overdrive. A hot flash engulfed her, which thankfully charred the butterflies which had been winging through her equally thrilled and nauseated belly, and she was suddenly hit with the inexplicable urge to run.

Unfortunately her feet seemed to have taken root.

A soft smile of recognition curved his wickedly sensual mouth and those ocean-colored eyes glittered with disbelief.

"Brownie?"

CHAPTER TWO

ON HIS WAY TO MEET a date in Charlotte, Jackson Harper, who was already running late, knew that he didn't have time to stop and help a stranded motorist.

Unfortunately, he couldn't *not* stop.

It had been hardwired into his brain, possibly even encoded into his DNA, *not* to drive by. His father had always been a huge proponent of the old you-reap-what-you-sow adage and, as such, he'd never missed an opportunity to help out a "neighbor" in need.

More often than not to their detriment.

His father, now retired, had been a misnomer—an honest mechanic—and it hadn't been unusual for customers to work out their debt cleaning the shop. Nor had it been out of the ordinary for his father to accept payment in the form of garden vegetables and the occasional piece of livestock.

As such, the minute he'd spied the vehicle with the hood up on the side of the road and the dainty little female peering under the hood, he'd known that he couldn't simply drive by. He'd phoned Celia and told her that he was going to be late, then had pulled over to offer his services.

Jackson had immediately recognized the coupe as one of the new retro Thunderbird's. He liked them well enough, but as a vintage car dealer, he had to admit that he much preferred the original 1955 version. Also, given that there was quite a bit of steam billowing from underneath the hood, he recognized that the problem was most likely due to a busted hose or faulty radiator.

What he hadn't anticipated was recognizing the owner of the vehicle.

Carley DeLuna.

This five-foot-two-inch blast from his past packed a sucker punch of shock that had almost sent him reeling back into the hood of his truck. Had the impact been literal rather than merely emotional, he would have undoubtedly been knocked off his feet like a comic book character, sprawled against the windshield.

As it was, it was all he could do to simply appear normal.

Unaffected.

When nothing could be further from the truth.

Carley DeLuna had been the love of his life and, while he had certainly moved on, she was the ruler by which he measured every other girl. So far no other woman had ever made the cut and, frankly, he'd accepted long ago that no one ever would.

There were times when Jackson felt like a fool for not being able to shake his high school sweetheart—

certainly other people had done so successfully—but he and Carley had been so much more to each other. As trite as it might sound, their relationship had been special. Unfortunately it hadn't been special enough to hold her here and he'd been too good a son to his father and his hometown to follow her to Charlotte.

He'd hoped that she'd make her mark and come back. In fact, he'd banked on it, otherwise he might have done things differently. In the end, though, he supposed everything had worked out as it should. For reasons he'd never understood—being a glutton for punishment, he supposed—he'd kept up with her via her parents. Though he'd stopped working at the garage years ago, they still called him when problems arose. No doubt that would embarrass her, Jackson thought, staring at the obviously successful woman she'd become.

She wore a blousy blush pink dress which clung to her petite frame in all the right places, a pair of chunky sandals à la *The Brady Bunch* and a little cream colored hat which would have been right at home in Mayberry. Vintage bohemian, Jackson decided, concluding that the look suited her perfectly. Her pretty brown eyes were just as expressive and heavily lashed as he remembered and despite the hat, he could still discern her trademark chestnut curls.

"Brownie?" he asked again unnecessarily.

Carley cleared her throat and her rose-bud lips formed a shaky smile. "Hi, Jack."

"Wow," he said for lack of anything better. "It's, uh… It's been a long time." Too long.

She nodded. "It has," she replied, staring at him as though she couldn't quite believe her eyes. She chuckled and gave her head a little shake. "I, uh— *Wow*. How've you been?"

"Doing fine," he told her, which was for the most part true. "You?"

"Good." She gestured over her shoulder. "Well, I was until a few minutes ago, anyway. My *new* car decided to die on me."

Jackson felt a smile tug at his lips. "Yeah, I noticed that."

"Still a good guy, I see."

"I try to be," he said, warming at the compliment. "I learned from the master."

She dimpled. "How is your dad?"

"He's great. Retired now."

"And your mom?"

Jackson tilted his head back and laughed. "She's great. She's the mayor."

Carley's eyes widened and she gasped. "No!"

He'd found it hard to believe as well. His mother had always been the type to offer her services but never her opinion. When she'd announced to him and his sister that she planned to run for office, they both nearly keeled over in shock.

Jackson nodded. "Oh, yeah she is," he confirmed. "She's a natural."

Shaking her head in amazement, Carley sighed. "Wow. Sounds like things have changed."

"For the better, I think," Jackson told her. "But we've missed you around here."

A wash of pink stole over her cheeks. "Thanks," she murmured.

Since she'd asked about his family, it only seemed right that he should reciprocate the gesture. "How are your parents doing?"

Carley forced a smile. "Fine," she said. "Same as always." She gestured toward her cell phone. "I would have called them, but…"

But she'd driven past the exit and the chances of them having a way to come and get her were slim. He understood both her reasoning and her embarrassment. Still, embarrassment aside, they were her parents. She needed to accept them for who they were and be done with it. He could tell from the look on her face, the set of her mouth and shoulders that, despite everything she'd accomplished, she hadn't managed to do that yet. She'd be so much happier if she could, Jackson thought. In the meantime, she was just setting herself up for disappointment.

"Would you like me to take a look?" he asked.

She offered a grateful smile. "Are you sure you don't mind?"

He grinned at her. "Not at all. I wouldn't have stopped otherwise."

Carley led him around to the front of the vehicle and gestured wearily underneath the hood. "It made a noise, then steam started boiling out, so I pulled over."

Jackson braced his hands on the front of the car and peered around. "Had it overheated?"

A line emerged between her delicately arched brows. "Er... I don't think so."

Meaning that she hadn't been looking at the gauges. He smiled, for whatever reason, finding that adorable. It was easy enough to see the problem. The antifreeze and water pooled beneath the car indicated that it was as he first suspected—a bad radiator. After a minute, he told her as much. "I'm assuming it's still under warranty?"

She nodded, absently chewing her bottom lip. "Yeah. I'll need to have it towed to the dealership where I bought it in Charlotte." She shot him a quick look. "Not to say that I don't think that you're capable of fixing it, but part of the purchase price was the warranty and I just—"

"No worries," he interrupted her, mildly perturbed that she'd just assumed that he was still working for his father. What? he wondered. Was it his old truck? He kept it out of preference, not out of necessity. But of course she had no way of knowing that because clearly she hadn't bothered to keep up with him the way that he had with her. He summoned a smile. "I don't fix cars anymore."

"Oh?"

The one word begged the question what do you do now, but rather than tell her the truth—that he was a vintage car dealer whose client list included a popular late-night TV host and a certain charismatic governor— Jackson decided against it. Instead, prodded by some perverse devil, he nodded, stroked his chin and said, "Yeah, I've got a little used-car business now."

Her smile faltered. "Oh. That's— That's great."

While not directly patronizing, she clearly did not think that it was great. Evidently being a used-car salesman ranked below being a mechanic in her book. While anyone else might have come to the conclusion that she was a social snob, Jackson knew better. He knew her history, knew her family and knew that poverty had skewed her perception of standards beyond the norm. Still, he couldn't help but find himself a little annoyed. Would she ever learn to simply be happy with what she had?

Furthermore, Jackson didn't have to check his watch to know that the service department at the Ford dealership was already closed. Also, since it was Friday, he imagined it would be Monday or later before they could even start on it. From her slightly annoyed expression, she'd reached the same conclusion.

He carefully lowered the hood. "Listen, why don't you call a tow truck and I'll give you a ride home?"

"Oh, you don't have to do that," she said. She toed a piece of gravel and slid him a careful look. "I imagine your wife is waiting for you to get home."

Her blatant fishing for his marital status made him feel marginally better and he chewed the inside of his cheek to hide his smile. "If I had a wife, I'm sure that would be true. But seeing as I'm still single, it's fine."

She bit the corner of her lip. "It's Friday night. Don't you have plans?"

"None that can't be canceled to help out an old friend."

Carley considered him for a moment, her brown eyes twinkling. "Then I would very much appreciate your assistance." She winced. "Home's in Charlotte, though. Are you sure you don't mind making the drive?"

"I was headed there, anyway."

She waited, presumably for him to elaborate, but Jackson didn't. Since she hadn't bothered to wonder about him over the past ten years, it sure as hell wouldn't hurt her to wonder about a few things now, would it?

"Well, in that case, thank you."

"Gather your things and lock it up," he told her. "We can wait in my truck until your tow arrives."

She did as he instructed, then fell in beside him as they walked back to his truck. "This looks like the same Chevy you used to have."

He opened the door for her, purposely crowded into her personal space and grinned at her as she climbed inside. "That's because it *is* the same Chevy I used to have."

They'd fogged up the windows more times than he could count, made love for the first time—both his and hers—on the front seat, not to mention against the door and in the bed, with the aid of the tailgate.

He had the privilege of watching those melting caramel eyes turn dark with remembered heat.

This old truck was more than a mere form of transportation. Aside from the fact that he and his father had restored it for his sixteenth birthday, it was a trophy, a rolling sentimental tribute to her and what they'd had.

And she'd just climbed back into the cab.

And he was a moron, Jackson thought as he closed the door and rounded the hood. A stupid sappy moron to think that he'd ever be able to keep her there.

CHAPTER THREE

IF SEEING JACKSON Harper hadn't managed to knock her off her feet, then learning that she was sitting in the same old truck she'd given him her virginity in certainly shouldn't shake her up.

But it did.

Memories of long conversations and longer drives, steamy kisses and desperate, reckless, heart-breakingly pure and innocent lovemaking. God, Carley thought now. They'd been invincible. They'd had no concept of time or the future or actually growing up. It had been about living solely for the moment, making grandiose plans. Her lips quirked. Looking back, Carley had been more about making plans and Jackson had merely been indulging her.

Nevertheless, Carley couldn't deny the secret thrill that whipped through her belly as a result of being back in this truck with Jackson. Honestly, if he cranked the engine and an Air Supply song came on the radio, she'd probably suffer a minor heart attack, thinking she'd stepped back in time. Funny how songs had the power to evoke old memories. Her gaze slid to him as he slipped into the driver's seat, lingered over his woefully familiar profile. And even funnier how time had done nothing to dull the pining ache in her heart…or the swift surge of attraction currently tingling through her veins. She let go a small sigh.

Unfortunately he hadn't been the guy for her ten years ago and, even though he was single—she couldn't help mining for that little nugget of information—he wasn't the kind of guy she was looking for now. She inwardly cringed at the uncharitable thought, but knew it was true. Jackson had graduated from fixing used cars to selling them and, while she knew he provided a genuine service people needed, he was still clearly *content*.

Carley had been many things over the years, but could honestly say that *content* had never been one of them. She'd always celebrated each goal by setting a new one. She was focused, driven even. She knew that about herself. Embraced it, accepted it, and only wished she could find someone equally motivated. She'd tried dating guys with less ambition and it was the same story every time. They'd all eventually grown tired of her successes outpacing their own.

Curiously, she and Sam and Abby had been talking about this very thing just last week. They kept a quarterly appointment in Manhattan to catch up on everything and the main topic of this past lunch-therapy session had been about the shortage of appropriate men. Like her, Sam and Abby were both in the top of their fields and wanted a man who was, as well. It had gotten so bad that they made a pact, swearing off unsuitable men and, if memory served, she'd specifically scrubbed a used-car salesman from her list.

Of course, that had been before she'd run into *this one* again.

Jackson leaned across the seat, crowding her—purposely, she suspected, the opportunistic wretch—then opened the glove box and handed her a phone book.

She blinked, looked alternately at him, then the book.

A wry smile caught the corner of his mouth. "You'd wanted to call a tow truck," he reminded her.

"Right," Carley said, feeling a blush sting her cheeks. She quickly thumbed through the book, found a number and placed the call. Meanwhile, Jackson had pulled out his cell phone and was making a call, as well. Since he hadn't gone to the trouble to get out of the truck, she assumed that her blatant eavesdropping was expected. She watched him from the corner of her eye and waited for someone to pick up on the other end of her own line.

"Celia? Hey, it's Jackson. Listen, I'm afraid I'm going to have to cancel on you."

Celia, eh? Carley thought. He'd said he was headed to Charlotte anyway. Did she live there? Carley wondered, annoyed by the instant flare of jealously that made her fingers inexplicably tighten on her phone. Honestly, it was none of her concern. She had no business worrying about who he did or did not—

"Hello? Hello? Is anyone there?"

Carley started. "Er…yes. Sorry," she mumbled

sheepishly, angling herself away from him. Dammit, she'd been so intent listening to his conversation that she hadn't been participating in her own. She quickly gave the man on the line directions and arranged for the tow. By the time she'd finished her phone call, Jackson had completed his and was staring at her with a humiliatingly humorous smile. He'd known precisely what she'd been doing and had obviously caught her at it.

"Sorry you had to cancel your date," she said, confronting the elephant in the room rather than pretending that she hadn't heard.

"No problem," he said with a lazy shrug.

"The tow company has a guy about thirty minutes out. Maybe if he hurries, you can take me to Charlotte, then catch up with your friend."

She felt his gaze slide over her features, linger on her lips. "I *am* catching up with a friend."

"You know what I meant," she said, resisting the urge to squirm. "I hate that I've ruined your evening."

He chuckled low. "Seeing you is the best thing that's happened to me in a long time," he told her. "Trust me. My evening is far from ruined."

Oy. If he kept saying things like that, she was going to be in big trouble. Of the tear-his-clothes-off-we-can-make-this-work sort. Been there, done that, had the scar tissue on her heart to prove it. Was it getting hot in here? Carley wondered, pulling her dress away from her chest.

"You said you were going to Charlotte. Is that where

she's from?" Better to talk about this other woman than to envision being her, Carley decided.

"Yes."

"Is it serious?"

He chuckled. "As serious as seeing her once every couple of months can be, I suppose. What about you? I noticed you aren't wearing a ring either."

Carley shook her head. "Nah. No time for romance. My career keeps me pretty busy."

Jackson nodded consideringly. "That's what I've heard."

From her parents no doubt, Carley thought. She couldn't imagine any other source, particularly considering there was no one left in Summertown she kept in close contact with. Her one good friend had moved to Texas several years ago. She and Shelley still maintained contact, but they rarely spoke of their old hometown. Shelley had been a "projects" child, too, and had been equally eager to dust Summertown dirt from her feet.

"Vintage clothing, right?"

On firmer ground, Carley swallowed and nodded. "Right. I've got a little boutique in Charlotte."

"Your mom mentioned that you'd coordinated several red carpet ensembles as well," he said, seemingly impressed. "You don't have to be modest. Sounds like you're doing well."

She was, dammit, and being able to share her success with him was a singularly unique experience. He, of all people, knew how desperately driven she'd been to make her mark. Letting him know that her dreams had come to fruition was curiously like having them come full circle. She'd missed that, Carley realized now. The friendship, the camaraderie. Granted she had Sam and Abby, but Jackson was a friend woven so tightly into the fabric of her past—he'd been there when her dreams were born—that telling him gave her an excited joy she hadn't experienced in a long time.

She laughed softly and turned to face him more fully in the truck. "I *am*," she confirmed. "Way better than I ever expected, to be honest with you."

He slung an arm across the back of the seat. "Does it make you happy? Do you enjoy your work?"

"I do," she said, without the smallest hesitation. "Oh, there are times it can be as frustrating as any job, I suppose. But, on the whole…" She nodded, mulling it over. "Yeah, it definitely makes me happy."

He shrugged. "Then that's all that ultimately matters, right?"

"I suppose so," she said, sighing softly. "What about you? Does your work make you happy?" She couldn't imagine anyone being happy with saying they were a used-car salesman, but she supposed it took all kinds.

A hint of something that looked a bit like mischief flashed in his blue-green gaze, but it was gone so quickly Carley was inclined to believe she'd imagined it. "Selling used cars, you mean?"

She nodded.

"Oh, yeah. When I pair the right car up with the right buyer—" A faraway expression entered his gaze and a slow, almost magical smile curled his lips. "Yeah, it definitely makes me happy."

If any other person had made that claim, Carley probably wouldn't have believed them, but she'd known Jackson Harper long enough to know that lying wasn't within his character. And faking that kind of genuine joy was impossible.

He was truly happy being a used-car salesman.

And for whatever reason, it was as wonderful as it was disheartening. She shouldn't care, Carley told herself. What was it to her, so long as he was happy? Honestly, who was she to say he would have been happier doing something else?

All true, all rational *nonjudgmental* arguments.

And yet a small part of her couldn't help but rail against his decision, to think it was a complete waste of his talents. He was a smart, decent guy who'd had the potential to be anything he'd wanted to be! He could have been a rocket scientist, a stockbroker, a doctor even.

And out of every career field he could have gone into, he'd had to choose the one with possibly *the* most seedy connotation imaginable? A used-car salesman?

She smiled when she wanted to whimper. "That's great, Jack. I'm happy for you." Not a lie, per se. She was happy that he was happy. What sort of a person would she be otherwise? She'd just wanted more for him.

His gaze probed hers and a somewhat sad smile

turned his lips. "Well, it's not as glamorous a career as yours," he finally said. "But it's a living."

Somewhat puzzled by his expression, Carley merely nodded. Judging from the designer watch fastened upon his wrist, he was making a pretty decent living, she thought, intrigued. In her business it paid to recognize labels and he was sporting a couple of fairly pricey ones. Quite honestly, she wouldn't have imagined that anyone in his line of work could afford those things, but clearly he was doing better for himself than many of his counterparts.

An awkward silence ensued, making her wish that they hadn't talked about careers after all. Money always changed the status quo and regardless how happy Jackson's business made him, the fact that she out-earned him was clearly making him uncomfortable. Just another reason why things would have never worked out between them, Carley reminded herself, feeling her chest tighten uncomfortably.

Jackson checked the rearview mirror. "Ah. Looks like your tow has arrived."

A thought struck her. "I could hitch a ride to Charlotte with him, you know." She didn't want to, of course. But being with Jackson was wreaking havoc with her head—not to mention other parts of her body—and she wasn't sure this continued proximity was entirely good for her.

He shot her a smile and scratched his temple in mock perplexity. "Then who would fix my dinner?"

She chuckled, ridiculously relieved that he'd lightened the moment, and cocked her head. "You want me to cook for you?"

"It's the least you can do."

Now that was certainly an interesting way to wrangle a dinner invitation, Carley thought, impressed at his ingenuity. And it was *so* like Jackson. She felt a smile stretch across her lips, then heaved a faux put-upon sigh. "I guess I can feed you," she said begrudgingly.

He winked at her. "Or better yet, we could feed each other."

And with that singularly pulse-pounding comment, he opened the door and swung out of the truck.

CHAPTER FOUR

JACKSON DIDN'T KNOW at what point he'd decided that dinner would be in order, but he was certainly glad now that he'd had that little stroke of genius. They currently sat on Carley's brick patio, enjoying a couple of grilled chicken salads she'd thrown together—the tomatoes and herbs from her little garden, no less—along with a fresh loaf of honey wheat bread she'd pulled from her bread maker when she'd gotten home.

For whatever reason, Jackson had pictured her living in a condo or apartment downtown—something barrenly contemporary with white walls, hard lines and big splashes of color. Something efficient. He'd imagined her using an address as a base, as a status symbol, but never a home.

He couldn't have been more wrong.

Her small Craftsman-style home located in the historic district had been meticulously restored and had been packed full of a nice blend of comfortable furniture, antiques and art deco style pieces. The scent of fresh bread had assailed him the instant he'd walked through the front door, forcing him to draw a deep breath in appreciation.

Looking somewhat embarrassed, she'd set her things down on a long trestle table by the door, then had given him the grand tour. Every room had been carefully arranged and showcased her intriguing sense of style… most particularly her bedroom.

Rather than using a traditional suite of furniture, she'd built the room around a pair of enormous antique mahogany arched doors, inlaid with stained glass, as her headboard. Pale light glowed from behind the bed, illuminating the stained glass. It was striking, for lack of a better word and when he'd quizzed her about the choice, she'd said the doors had been salvaged from an old Mexican church.

Knowing that had made his next thoughts particularly blasphemous, because he'd instantly imagined tumbling her into that bed, stripping her naked and watching the various shades of color in the glass play off her creamy bare skin. To his everlasting delight, he got the distinct impression that she was having equally depraved thoughts about him because her gaze had taken on a slightly drunken look, and she'd licked her bottom lip and made a little sound low in her throat which had sounded suspiciously like a whimper. Then she'd hustled him out of the room, prattling on about getting to the kitchen and was salad okay with him.

It was a far different conversation to the one that had preceded them to Charlotte, that was for damned sure. Things had been tense there for a few minutes when he'd told her that he had a "little used-car business." Though she hadn't uttered an unkind word, and was genuinely happy that he was content, he felt her underlying disappointment as keenly as if she'd slapped him with it.

She'd expected more out of him, had wanted more for him. But she was still apparently unable to understand that, while she might have a legitimate claim for knowing what was right for *her*—what would ensure *her* happiness—she wasn't necessarily qualified to make that decision for other people.

If nothing else, she should have learned that lesson from her parents. Jackson knew that she'd offered to buy a little house near the town square for them, but they'd flatly refused. Though she couldn't understand it, her parents were happy in their apartment. It was the only life they'd known and they weren't interested in changing it. Would it be the life he'd choose? No. But, again, it wasn't up to him and, as his father often said, you couldn't help people who didn't want to help themselves.

At any rate, the drive to her house had been unbelievably enjoyable. They'd caught up a little more, and quickly found the familiar rhythm of conversation they'd shared, discussing current events, movies they'd seen, books they'd read. He and Carley had never lacked things in common and it was refreshing and reassuring that things hadn't changed.

Pleasantly full, he leaned back in his chair and studied her. A play of twinkling lights glittered from a decorative tree behind her, picking up the golden highlights in her hair. Whatever makeup she'd applied this morning had faded, leaving her fresh-faced and gorgeous. Just looking at her made his chest ache and his groin throb. Nobody had ever had that kind of effect on him. No one, with the exception of Carley, had ever engaged his heart *and* his libido. God, how he'd missed that, Jackson thought. He'd had sex dozens of times over the past ten years, but he hadn't made love to a woman since he'd been with her.

If it wasn't so depressing, it would be pathetic.

Carley sent him a questioning look. "What are you thinking? Or do I want to know?" she asked with guarded suspicion.

"I've just missed you," he said simply, surprising them both with the simple truth.

She swallowed and offered a sweet smile that tugged at his heartstrings. "Oh."

"Oh?" he repeated, feigning injury. "That's it? I tell you that I've missed you, Brownie, and all you can say is oh? Come on," he teased. "Gimme something. It's pretty damned lonely out here on this limb."

A soft tinkling chuckle bubbled up her throat. "Still shameless, I see,"

"Still stingy with your feelings, I see," he joked.

"Stingy with my feelings? I was never stingy with my feelings with you!" she cried, outraged.

"Well, you weren't exactly forthright, either." He gave his head a regretful woe-is-me shake. "I was always telling you how much you meant to me—" He frowned, made a face of resigned disappointment.

"Then I'd have to wait like a mongrel at the butcher's cart for you to throw me a bone."

She inhaled sharply and her eyes widened in shock. "Throw you a bone?" she repeated. "You've lost your mind! I doted upon you! I treated you like royalty, you ungrateful jerk."

He laughed. "And who could forget those little pet names?" he lamented fondly. "Jerk. Idiot. Fool." He sighed dramatically. "Ahhh…those were the days."

Carley merely shook her head and smiled. "Well, one thing certainly hasn't changed."

"And what's that?" Who would have thought picking a little fight with her again would have been this much fun? Jackson couldn't recall when he'd had a better time.

She snorted. "You're still full of shit."

A burst of laughter broke up in his throat. He sighed and, smiling, inclined his head. "There is that."

She peeked at him beneath lowered lashes. "But I've missed you, too."

A balloon of joy rapidly inflated in his chest, causing other parts of him south of his waistband to inflate as well. "See there? That wasn't so hard, was it?"

"I suppose not," she said grudgingly.

He laughed again, strangely both wired and content. "This is nice," he said. "Sort of like old times, eh?"

"Yeah. You'll have to come by and see me when you're up this way again." She made a face. "Well, unless you're in town to see Celia, of course, in which case that would be in poor taste."

So she'd listened closely enough to catch Celia's name, then? Jackson thought, ridiculously pleased. Jealous? After all these years? Could she still be nursing a heartache, too? he wondered. Oh, he'd detected the attraction and a certain fondness, that was for sure. But could it be more? Or was that merely wishful thinking on his part?

"Oh, that would definitely be in poor taste," he agreed, needling her. "I wouldn't dream of seeing both of you the same weekend."

She harrumphed and rolled her eyes. "How respectful," she said wryly. "It's nice to know I would merit my own tank of gas."

He cocked his head. "What can I say? I think a lot of you." Too true on many levels.

She leaned back in her chair. "Keep it up, smart ass, and I'll rescind the invitation."

"I told you things weren't serious with Celia, that I only saw her every couple of months."

She chewed the inside of her cheek, regarding him with a cocked brow. "Yes, you did. Just often enough to scratch an itch, I suspect."

Jackson laughed, surprised at her candor.

"Why do you think I offered to take a ride with the tow driver? I had sense enough to know what I was interrupting for you tonight."

"Then you ought to have sense enough to know that you were worth it."

She smiled and cast him a playful look. "I would be lying if I said that wasn't a bit gratifying."

"What about you?" Jackson asked, turning the tables on her, bracing himself for her answer because it was sure to wreak mortal hell with his temper. "Have you got a fallback guy who—" he had to stop and clear his throat "—occasionally scratches your itches?"

Her gaze tangled directly with his and a slow smile slid around her sexy lips. "I scratch my own itches."

Sweet mother of— Every last drop of moisture promptly evaporated from his mouth, and every ounce of blood made a beeline for his crotch. In a nanosecond of that ballsy comment, he was hard.

Looking curiously pleased with herself, Carley calmly stood and began clearing the dishes. "You're finished, right?" she said in a perfectly cordial tone, as though she hadn't just told him that she—

Dainty fingers, parting curls, legs wide open…

Jackson managed a nod, released a breath he didn't realize he'd been holding.

Oh, he was finished, all right, he thought with a futile sigh. He drained his wineglass, watched her heart-shaped rump swing in a hypnotizing rhythm as she walked back into the kitchen.

He was finished the moment he stepped out of his truck tonight and saw her standing there.

CHAPTER FIVE

CARLEY DIDN'T KNOW what the hell had possessed her to say such a thing—*I scratch my own itches*—but something about his self-satisfied smile had struck a nerve and she'd wanted to strike back.

Where it would hurt him.

The moment her comment had registered, she'd had the privilege of watching those clear blue-green eyes go a bit murky with desire, had watched him struggle to swallow and ultimately squirm in his chair. It didn't take a genius to figure out why, and the end result of her little comment was particularly gratifying. She snorted under her breath. He wouldn't see both her and Celia the same weekend? She rolled her eyes. Cocky, adorable jerk.

For reasons she knew better than to explore too deeply, the idea of him coming to town and seeing anyone other than her—having anyone other than her scratch his infernal itches—was absolutely *torturous*.

This, after only being in his company again for a few hours. The vicious grip of unwarranted jealousy was just as disproportionate as it was ridiculous. She had no claim on him. She'd given it up years ago to pursue a different life, one she was proud of. Carley stilled.

But if that were the case, then why did the idea of him walking back out of her life tonight weigh on her heart like an anchor of dread? Why did it make her sick to her stomach? Why was it, God help her, *unthinkable?*

She didn't want him to leave, dammit. *Ever,* a little voice added, much to her chagrin. Which was ridiculous when she knew things could never work out between them. Despite ten years of maturity, she was the same old driven Carley and he was the same old content Jackson. This was crazy and she was simply begging for more heartache.

And yet…she'd sat through the past few hours thinking about how desperately she wanted him to kiss her. And more. Much, much more. He'd always had the most remarkable mouth. Lips that were neither too thin nor too full, and just the perfect combination of soft and firm. And when he smiled…

Mercy.

She felt that grin in places it had no business affecting. It made her chest tighten, then lighten, and her toes curl in her shoes. It made her tingle. She let out a shuddering breath.

It made her hot.

She'd experienced a similar meltdown when she'd been showing him around her house—in her bedroom, in particular. With the exception of the house itself, Carley was most pleased with her bed.

She'd vacationed in Mexico year before last—alone, of course because Abby and Sam weren't able to get away—and her tour bus had made an unscheduled stop to repair a blown tire. It was then that she'd come across the church. Workers were swiftly dismantling the building and, aside from the fact that there was something sad about the small place's demise, she'd been drawn to the doors. She'd rescued them from a scrap heap and could have bought a round-trip ticket to Nepal for what it had cost her to ship them home. But she'd never regretted the rash decision.

Curiously enough, she remembered thinking at the time that Jackson, who'd always had an affinity for stained glass, would have liked them. Furthermore, while it was true that she did occasionally scratch her own itch, she'd left out one little niggling detail—he was always her inspiration.

Granted she'd met a few celebrities in her line of work who definitely cranked her tractor, but none had ever succeeded in putting it into gear the way the merest thought of Jackson Harper, with his easy smile and sexy laugh, could.

And Carley knew why.

Despite everything that had happened between them—the heartache and break-up and the different roads chosen—at the end of the day, Carley knew he was the only guy who'd ever truly loved her. A lump welled in her throat. He was the only person on this planet with the exception of her parents who'd ever wholeheartedly given a damn about her without having to.

Whether he still did or not remained to be seen, but she couldn't deny that knowing that Jackson Harper had loved her was probably one of the very best things that had ever happened to her.

He strolled in, carrying his plate. "Can I help?"

And he picked up after himself, Carley thought. Could a man be any more perfect?

His steps slowed and he shot her a cautious smile. "What are you grinning about?"

She chuckled, feeling like a moron. She shook her head. "Nothing."

He sidled closer. "It doesn't look like nothing. Come on. What's the deal?"

She shrugged. "You brought your plate in."

Confusion cluttered his brow. "Er...would you rather I left it outside?"

"Of course not," she said with an exasperated laugh.

"And that's it?" he asked, seemingly surprised. "*That's* what put that smile on your face?"

Smiling, Carley shrugged, but didn't say anything.

He shook his head in obvious bewilderment. "You're one easy-to-please woman. Here," he teased. "Let me give you another thrill. I'll *rinse* my plate, too."

"Smart ass."

He moved closer to her. "Maybe. But I'm a tidy smart ass."

And he was an absolutely beautiful smart ass, too, Carley decided as she released a shuddering breath. She loved the way he moved, unhurried yet confident, as though he were completely at ease in his own skin. Soft black curls clung behind the surprisingly delicate shell of his ear, drawing the eye to his unusually handsome profile. He was doing something as simple as rinsing off a plate and yet he couldn't have been any sexier.

God, how she'd missed him.

Her heart squeezed, aching with regret and longing and a melancholy sense of familiarity that made her wish that this night never had to end.

Jackson turned the faucet off, tucked his plate in the dishwasher, then leaned a hip against the counter and turned to look at her. Her heart jumped into an irregular rhythm. "It's getting late," he said. "I should probably be heading back."

Carley swallowed. Every part of her rebelled against the idea of him walking out of here tonight. For whatever reason—probably a combination of too much wine and an acute desire to be loved again, if only for a little while—she was hit with the overwhelming impression that she'd be squandering an irreplaceable opportunity. Of what sort, she wasn't entirely sure. She just knew that she didn't want him to leave. She wanted— *needed*—him to stay.

The problem was, she wasn't sure she could summon the courage to ask him to.

Carley fidgeted. "Are you working tomorrow?" she asked, figuring that Saturdays were a big day for used-car salesmen.

Jackson studied her thoughtfully and that careful

scrutiny made her scalp tingle. "No," he said. "I'm free until Sunday afternoon."

So undoubtedly he'd planned on spending the night with Celia, she concluded, irrationally jealous once more of the faceless woman who scratched his occasional itches.

"What about you?" he asked. "Are you working tomorrow?"

Carley's lips quirked in a wry smile. "No, and it's a good thing, considering I don't have any way of getting around." She made a mental note to call a rental company in the morning.

"So no plans, then?"

She looked up and her gaze tangled with his. Was it her imagination, or had he moved closer? "No," she said, emitting a little sigh.

"Then why don't I stay in town tonight—I'll check into a hotel—and we could do something together tomorrow?"

A thrill of happiness whipped through her, pushing her lips into a delighted grin. She resisted the childish urge to do a little happy dance. "Like what?"

He shrugged, lowered his voice and scooted in a little closer to her. A shiver tripped down her spine and those watercolor eyes fastened on to hers, causing a mini-tornado to whip through her midsection. "Doesn't matter to me, Brownie," he murmured softly. "I just want to spend some time with you."

Warm delight bloomed in her chest. That was

another thing that she'd always appreciated about him—right, wrong or indifferent, he was unfailingly honest. And if he could lay it all on the line, then she could too, Carley decided.

"I'd like that very much," she said. "And you can go to a hotel if you'd like…but you're more than welcome to stay here. I've got a spare room."

Not that she'd want him to sleep in it, of course, but…

A slow sexy smile eased across his lips and a wicked chuckle rose up his throat. "Unless you can lock it from the outside, sweetheart, I'm thinking that would be a risky move."

She offered a small shrug, deciding to crawl out on that limb beside him. "When the risk is worth the reward…"

Heat instantly flared in his gaze, turning it into a blue flame that had the singular ability to draw her closer. He slid the pad of his thumb over her bottom lip, causing her pulse to leap. "Are you asking me to spend the night?"

Her breath caught in her throat. Direct as always, right to the heart of the matter. "I don't want you to leave," Carley confessed, surprised at her own candor. She let go a breath. "So, yeah, I guess I am."

Jackson's gaze dropped to her lips, then jumped back up and tangled with hers. He framed her face with his hands, causing a shudder to work its way through her. Her lids fluttered shut against the remembered pleasure of his hands upon her skin and she was so moved, she felt her eyes water unexpectedly. He brushed his lips lightly over hers, snatching her breath, then said, very softly, his voice loaded with an emotion she couldn't name, "Then I'd be honored."

Then he kissed her again and emotion met desire…and life was suddenly brighter than it had been in years.

CHAPTER SIX

WITH EACH PASSING SECOND tonight, Jackson had been dreading the moment he would have to leave and desperately anticipating the moment he would kiss her. Now, as he stood in her kitchen, her woefully familiar body pressed to his, her sweet lips clinging to his, he couldn't believe his good fortune.

She hadn't wanted him to leave either.

And *thank God*, was all he could think, his relief making him melt into her, because the idea of getting into his truck and driving home or even going to a hotel for that matter had been…unimaginable. It had been ten long years since he'd seen Carley and, though he'd only been with her a few hours today, it had been long enough to realize that he could easily fall head over heels in love with her all over again—provided he'd ever stopped in the first place.

And kissing her now, feeling his chest expand with some sort of tingly sensation, every cell locked and loaded and desperately hungry for her, he knew that was a big *if*.

He felt her hands push into his hair, her fingers gently

knead his scalp and a hot quaking throb settled in his loins, pushing his dick dangerously close to the waistband of his jeans. Fire licked through his veins as her hot tongue explored his mouth. She suckled and probed, sought and retreated and with each sweep and each drugging caress he felt himself losing more and more control.

As if he'd ever had any to start with where Carley was concerned.

Tasting her was bittersweet, a homecoming, coupled with a depth of emotion he hadn't felt in years and a desperate urgency to plant himself between her legs that made him want to forego the bedroom and take her right where they stood. Her hands were all over him, enflaming him, burning away any vestiges of a sentimental seduction and leaving nothing but a charred urgency to make her his again, to make her forget about scratching her own itches or letting any other guy who might come after do it either.

She was his, damn it, and the overwhelming need to mark her as such pounded through him with a primal force that he had to act on by swiftly picking her up and hauling her toward the bedroom.

Carley gasped with delight, but clung to him all the same, raining enflaming kisses along his jaw and down the side of his neck.

"We aren't going to make it the bedroom if you don't cut that out," he warned, feeling a bead of moisture leak out of his dick.

"I don't have a problem with that," she whispered, then licked the shell of his ear.

A shudder worked its way through him and he had to grit his teeth. The couch loomed before him, a silent invitation, and it took every ounce of strength he possessed to bypass it and head into the hall.

In all honesty, he could have taken her in the kitchen against the damned refrigerator, could have made any spot in her house the perfect place to make love to her, but something about that bed and those doors, in particular… Call him romantic, but Jackson liked the symbolism.

Open doors, new beginnings, a threshold to a better future.

Furthermore it had been too long since he'd been with her and she deserved more than a quick, desperate tumble. He wanted to do her right—literally—and for that he needed a proper bed and a bit of perspective. He swallowed a groan of pleasure. None of which he was going to have if she didn't stop kissing his neck—his weak spot, which she undoubtedly remembered, the crafty witch.

He set her upon the bed, then slowly followed her down, purposely resetting the pace. Every part him longed for instant gratification—he couldn't wait to be between her thighs, to feel her greedy body clenching around him. But he'd waited too long for this reunion and the idea of spoiling it with urgency was simply out of the question. He wanted to taste and savor, to feel and be felt. He cupped her cheek, deepened the kiss and ate her sigh, feeling her melt into the mattress beneath him.

"Oh, Jack," she said. "I've missed you."

He licked a path down the side of her neck, then drew back and traced a half-heart on her cheek. "Ditto, Brownie," he said softly.

A slow smile dawned on her lips and she offered them up to his once more, then slid her hands down his back and began tugging his shirt from the waistband of his jeans. The first brush of her fingers against his bare skin made a storm of gooseflesh pelt up his spine.

And just like that, his good intentions flew out the window and the pace he'd set only seconds ago simply vanished in a rush of sensation so intense that time no longer mattered. All that mattered was touching her, tasting her, making love to her.

She wiggled beneath him and he heard the dull thud of her shoes hitting the floor, then she drew his shirt up over his head and tossed it aside. Her palms slid over his chest, mapping him wonderingly, even as her eyes went even darker with desire. Those beautiful brown curls lay fanned out beneath her, framing her face. Her lips were ripe and swollen from his kisses and if he'd ever seen anything so lovely, he couldn't recall it. She was hungry. For him. And he had every intention of letting her feast.

But not before he did.

Jackson kicked off his own shoes, then found the hem of her dress—which wasn't hard considering it had bunched up her legs—and quickly helped her out of it. Creamy, flawless skin. Bowtie mole above her right collar bone, just as he remembered.

God help him.

His gaze drifted down her ribcage, over her belly and he smiled when he noticed something different, something that hadn't been there ten years ago—a tiny purple butterfly hovered just above the top of her pink lacy panties on her right hip. Inked? Carley?

"Shocked, are you?" she asked, evidently pleased with herself.

"Pleasantly surprised," he corrected, drinking his fill of her as she lay below him.

A sheer pale pink bra covered her breasts, but couldn't disguise her tautened nipples. Puckered, just for him, he thought awed. He gently slipped a finger over the swell of one breast, had the pleasure of feeling her quiver beneath him, then bent low and drew the sweet bud into his mouth through the fabric.

She gasped and pushed her fingers into his hair, arching up against him in an unspoken primal invitation that made his dick jerk hard against his zipper. He smiled, then slowly popped the front clasp and nudged the cup aside. Beautiful, Jackson thought, simply beautiful. He lowered his head once more and sampled the other breast, suckling softly, drawing her farther into his mouth.

Evidently unable to allow him to torture her without reciprocating, Jackson felt her warm little hands slide down his back, then circle around to the snap of his jeans. In an instant she'd worked the button loose from its closure, then just was swiftly lowered the zipper. No longer a prisoner in his pants, he felt himself spring free, jutting instinctively into her waiting hand.

He set his jaw as she palmed him, then slid a hand down her quivering belly until he found the top of her panties. He traced the edge, following the seam down the side, then deftly slipped his fingers underneath the damp fabric.

Hot. Wet. Wonderful.

She gasped, then whimpered as he parted her curls, carefully dragging his fingers back and forth, glazing her folds more evenly. She squirmed beneath his touch, and increased her own ministrations, sliding a finger around the engorged head of his penis. She caught a drip of moisture on her thumb, then coated him with it.

It distracted him enough to leave her breasts and lick a bisecting path down her belly. He paused to kiss her butterfly, then quickly positioned himself between her legs. One careless tug and her panties were off and she was wet and bare and pink before him.

"I don't know about scratching this itch," Jackson told her, blowing softly against her weeping flesh. "But licking it ought to do the trick, eh?"

She groaned and threw her head back against the bed. "Jack—"

He fastened his mouth upon her, suckling and stroking her with his tongue. The scent of Woman filled his nostrils and the taste of her exploded on his tongue, rich and full and wicked and addictive. She was soft—

so very soft—and he slid a finger into her slick heat, delighted when he felt her clench around him.

Carley fisted her hands in the sheets, thrashing beneath his intimate kiss. "You've got to— Oh, you mustn't— Son of a—"

He cupped his tongue over the sweet bud nestled at the crest of her curls and tongued her harder. A cry tore from her arched throat, then she looked up at him.

"Not now," she pleaded, her face flushed. "I want you inside of me when I—"

She didn't have to finish. He knew exactly what she meant. She wanted him inside her when she came, which was fine with him, because he couldn't imagine any other place he'd rather be.

Ever.

Jackson kicked his jeans completely off, finished shucking his boxers, then knelt between her legs once more.

Her gaze locked with his and she lifted her hips, nudging him against her hot, wet folds. He set his jaw so hard he could have sworn he heard a tooth crack, then in one long, deliberate thrust, he seated himself fully inside her.

His world shifted.

Carley smiled with joyous relief and instantly tightened around him, claiming him, Jackson thought. A blistering, quaking heat rolled over his body and his heart gave a weird little flutter. It was almost as if an electric current started in the arches of his feet and swept over him, making every muscle lock and his scalp tingle.

He looked down into her flushed, beaming face and felt his chest bloom with an emotion he'd only known in her arms.

Love.

And just like that, he was hers again.

He just hoped like hell she'd want him this time.

CHAPTER SEVEN

JACKSON HARPER. Naked. In her bed. Poised between her thighs.

Again.

Oh, sweet mercy, dreams *did* come true.

Carley rocked her hips forward, felt a euphorically relieved smile shape her lips as he bumped at her center, then slowly, deliberately pushed into her. Her breath left her in an equally deliberate whoosh, as though his mere presence inside her body was pushing it out of her lungs.

She instinctively tightened around him, felt pleasure arch through her womb and radiate outward until her limbs were weak and there was no room for another thought in her head.

She slid her hands all over him, determinedly drugging herself with the touch of him beneath her palms. She mapped and explored…intriguing muscle, ridges and valleys, a male nipple, corded neck, that sweet spot she knew that drove him crazy behind his ear. He was hot and hard, thrilling and dark and she wanted him—craved him—as she'd never wanted another man.

Jackson withdrew, then plunged back in and she met

his thrust, rose up and took it, and then begged for more, increasing the tempo. She couldn't get enough—couldn't feel enough of him—and fueled the fever running through her veins by drawing her legs back and wrapping them tightly around his waist.

He smiled and pounded harder, his tight balls slapping against her aching flesh. A flash of white heat burned through her loins, heralding the first quickening of climax. Carley fisted her feminine muscles around him, trying to hold him inside her, relishing every delicious draw and drag between their joined bodies.

He reached down and laced his fingers through hers, a tender gesture in the midst of mindlessness and the feel of his entire body pressed against hers—sensitive nipples abrading his chest, the hot hard length of him buried deeply inside of her, his scent, something musky and Male and uniquely Jackson—stole over her.

He hammered harder and faster, and then faster still, then he bent down and pulled an aching nipple deep into the hot cavern of his mouth. As though connected by an invisible string, the thin bow which had been holding her together suddenly gave way and the raining release of a climax stole through her, sucking her under, then lifting her up.

Her mouth opened in a soundless scream, her back bowed off the bed as the brunt of it ripped through her and with each forceful pulsation around him, the pleasure magnified, ultimately making her eyes water and her chest ache with joy.

Five seconds later Jackson joined her in paradise. She heard him groan, felt him go rigid, then a long keening roar tore from his throat and he buried himself so deeply inside of her she had the fanciful impression that he'd just nudged her heart. Why else would it be in her throat? Why else would she be clinging so tightly to him, caught between the wild urge to laugh and to weep?

He collapsed, neatly rolling them both to the side and carefully withdrew from her. She missed him at once, but felt marginally better as he tucked her head beneath his chin and held her close. How she'd missed being here, Carley thought, wrapped so protectively in his arms.

He pressed a gentle kiss to her head. "That was…" He paused, seemingly at a loss.

Carley smiled and laid a kiss against his chest. "I know."

"I've *missed* you," he said again.

Carley chuckled. "You've told me. I've missed you, too."

"No, it's—" He gave his head a small shake. "I don't think I knew just how much until tonight. Does that make sense?"

Carley swallowed. It certainly did. She'd missed him as well, but the ache had never been keener than when she'd seen him again, and the thought that he was going to leave… "It does," she said. "I feel the same way. Why do you think that I told you that I didn't want you to leave?"

"Because you wanted my body," he said deadpan voice.

She gasped, outraged and propped herself up on her elbow to study him. "I don't think I was the only person here lusting after a body tonight." She cast him a shrewd look. "You don't think I knew what you were doing with that *hard lean* toward the glove box in your truck tonight?"

He chuckled. "Busted. What can I say? I wanted to hug you the second I'd realized it was you on the side of the road, but I didn't know how you'd feel about that, so I kept my distance."

It had been merely hours after that breakdown on the freeway, and now they were lying in her bed, naked and sweating and reeking with the scent of hot, frantic sex. And he'd been afraid to hug her? "I can see that you did that," she replied drolly.

She felt his laugh vibrate her side. "You know what I mean," he told her, absently stroking her upper arm.

"What are we going to do tomorrow?" Carley asked. "Did you have anything in mind?"

Her lips *and* toes curled. "What about *aside* from this?"

"Whatever you want to, Brownie. I am yours to command."

She perked up. "Really?" she asked significantly.

His wary chuckle made her smile. "In a manner of speaking."

"When do I get to start being in charge?"

He pulled a face and scratched the side of his head. "Haven't you always been in charge?"

She laughed again. "Not if my memory can be trusted."

"Then it's clearly faulty," he said matter-of-factly.

Ha, Carley thought. She grunted but didn't say anything.

"You sound awful eager to start bossing me around. What exactly is it that you'd like to do?"

Stay right here with you for the rest of my life, Carley thought. *Tell the rest of the world to simply go away. Not worry about jobs or money or ambition or lack thereof. Just be left all alone—with Jackson.* She let go a small sigh.

That's what she'd like to do.

And if wishes were horses, then beggars would ride. Because all of the above was out of the question. They hadn't been able to make it happen at eighteen, when nothing had seemed impossible. She knew better than to even dare to dream that it could happen now. Even still, she couldn't make herself let him go, couldn't convince herself that being with him was anything short of right.

Carley swallowed a small sigh. "What do I want to do right now, you mean?"

"Right now's a start," he said, chuckling softly.

She kissed his chest, slid her hand over his belly. "Right now I'd like to take a shower."

He hummed appreciatively under his breath. "I could easily accommodate that command."

Her lips quirked. "That almost sounds like you intend to pick and choose which commands you follow."

"If that was the case, it would be criminally stupid of me to tell you, wouldn't it?"

"Jack," she chided, feigning exasperation. "I knew you were only giving me the illusion of power."

"Oh, it's no illusion," he told her. "You're just going to have to use your imagination when it comes to wielding it."

She let her hand drift lower along his belly, felt his body shudder. She gently stroked him. "Like this, you mean?"

A choked groan erupted from his throat. "Th-that's a start."

"I think I'm having an allergic reaction," she said.

"What?"

She leaned forward and kissed him, a long slow siege that made her womb grow all hot and muddled again. His dick swelled gratifyingly in her hand. "I'm itching," she said meaningfully.

He chuckled. "You want me to scratch you?"

"No. I want you to lick me. All over. Again."

His voice, when he spoke, was a bit strangled. "What about that shower?"

She tugged him up and led him toward her bathroom. "What about it?"

A wicked laugh bubbled up his throat and without warning, he scooped her up again. "Come on, Brownie. Let's see what we can do about that itch."

CHAPTER EIGHT

JACKSON WATCHED Carley negotiate the traffic behind him in the rental car that they'd just picked up for her—another retro, this one a pale green Mustang convertible. She wore another one of those funky hats like the one she'd had on yesterday and those big oversize sunglasses that were so popular with the Hollywood set. She might as well be tooling down Rodeo Drive, he thought. She certainly looked the part.

He grinned, feeling ridiculously happy.

She did that to him. *She* made him happy.

Jackson had awoken this morning in her big warm bed, a soft rump pressed against his loins and a plump breast beneath his hand. There'd been a smile on his face before he'd even opened his eyes and he'd simply lain there as dawn painted the world outside her window in the first rays of pinkish-orange light and absorbed the rightness of the moment. He'd listened to the sound of her breathing and had been momentarily awed to realize that they were in sync, each inhalation perfectly in tune with the other.

Last night had been beyond incredible, past anything

he'd ever experienced or would ever experience again. Though he knew it was insane to think that they could simply pick up where they'd left off, that's exactly what it had felt like. Time had passed, yes, but his feelings for her had never changed, and despite her thirst for success and what she deemed a better life, Jackson knew her feelings for him had never changed either.

She was still as much in love with him as he was with her.

He'd seen it in those warm brown eyes, heard it in every word she'd said, every laugh and teasingly fond smile. More importantly, he'd felt it in her touch. Making love had laid her bare and she'd shown him time and time again all during the night just how much she cared.

The question now was, would it be enough? Enough to make her stop equating money with happiness? Enough to make her realize that if she'd only let him, he could make her happier than any of her goals. They were cold comfort, dammit. She ought to know that by now.

Jackson didn't want her to walk back out of his life again and disappear for another ten years. They'd wasted too much time as it was. He wanted a commitment, the whole package.

He wanted her.

Thankfully today had been fabulous, with only one tense reminder of what she presumed was a distance in their economic status. Jackson had gotten a call on his cell from a certain high-profile client who'd purchased several classic cars from him. It was the same client who'd be arriving in Summertown tomorrow afternoon. Jackson couldn't avoid the call because he'd needed to confirm the appointment.

Carley had pretended to study a collection of vintage hats—they'd been in one of many antique shops and junk stores he'd watched her plunder through today— but he'd known that she'd been listening intently.

"Sounds like you've made another sale," she'd said when he'd ended the call. "Congratulations."

And while he'd known that she was sincere, he'd still detected a bit of melancholy disappointment in her voice that he found extremely disheartening, not to mention, were he completely honest, annoying. He didn't like being the object of her pity, particularly when it wasn't deserved. He made a damned fine living, thank you very much.

He didn't have any idea exactly how much money she made, but he could easily total her assets and make a ball-park estimate. He knew that if her bottom line was better than his, it couldn't be by too much.

Though it was purely selfish on his part, he was looking forward to seeing the look on her face when he finally confessed the truth about his "little used-car business." He'd started to come clean earlier this afternoon, but for whatever reason, hadn't been able to summon the nerve.

In the first place, it had belatedly occurred to him that she probably wasn't going to appreciate his slight misrepresentation of his business. If fact, he fully expected her to be pissed. Ultimately though, he knew she'd get over it. She'd be too happy for him to do otherwise.

And secondly, call him a sentimental fool, but he wanted her to love and accept him for who he was, not what sort of business he was in. If they made this work—and God how he hoped that they would—he wanted to be sure, to *know*, that Carley was with him because she loved him, not because of some trumped-up notion of his success. If she found out about his vintage car business beforehand and things worked out between them, he'd never know for sure what her true feelings were. Furthermore—and possibly more importantly—neither would she.

Jackson slowed his truck, allowing her to come around him so that she could pull into her driveway first. She twinkled her fingers at him and then blew him a kiss as she passed, making him chuckle underneath his breath.

Ah, home, he thought, thinking that if things worked out between them, he wouldn't mind living here with her. Not that he didn't love his own house, but she'd clearly invested more of herself here than he had in his own place. And, as far as his business went, he could just as easily handle most things from here as he could in Summertown. It was only an hour's commute. Funny how that had seemed like such a huge distance ten years ago. But now…Jackson grinned, exited the truck and sauntered toward her. Now it seemed perfectly doable.

Just like her.

He'd been stealing kisses all day, hadn't been able to keep his hands off her and, though he had a wonderful time watching her in her element and actually pilfering through the various stores of her trade with her this afternoon, he couldn't wait to get back here.

Because he wanted her again.

And again and again and again.

Making up for lost time? Who knew? He just knew that he couldn't get enough of her, couldn't think beyond creamy thighs, pink flesh and plump pouting breasts. His dick instantly swelled at the mental image. Hell, Jackson thought, at the rate he was going, he'd be lucky to get her into the house. His gaze slid to the convertible.

"Not in the yard, for chrissakes," she admonished, evidently following his train of thought.

Jackson pinned her against the door, lowered his head and captured her sweet mouth in a hot kiss. "Who said anything about the yard? I was thinking about the car."

She made a purr of pleasure, looped her hands around his neck. "The car is in the yard, genius. And I have neighbors who would be positively scandalized. Come," she said imperiously. "Let's go inside."

Smiling, Jackson followed her. "You're taking this 'yours to command' thing a little far, don't you think?" She'd been giving him orders all day, clearly enjoying wielding her power over him.

She chuckled, then inserted the key into the lock and opened the door. "Wishing you hadn't told me that I could?"

"No," he said. "I was just hoping I'd get some interesting orders."

He'd barely made it through the door before Carley whirled and pushed him back into it. She nipped at his earlobe and sighed, causing a little quake to move through him. "Interesting, eh? How's this? *Take me.*"

A broken chuckle bubbled up his throat and he lifted her off her feet, delighted when she made a little "oh" of surprise. "Now that's more like it," he growled, setting her on top of her kitchen table. Baking bread scented the air—rosemary this time—and the afternoon sun beamed through the window over the sink, painting the kitchen in soft golden light.

Kissing wildly, she unsnapped his pants while he hiked up her dress. Jackson smiled when he found only bare skin where her panties should be. "No panties?"

"Saves time," she said, panting, her hand closing around him.

And she was efficient too, he thought as a strangled laugh broke loose in his throat. He found her lips once more, tangled his tongue around hers and sighed into her mouth as she guided him toward her center. She was hot, slick and ready and he entered her in one fierce stroke.

She cried out, clenched around him and lashed her arms more tightly around his neck. Her breath seemed to catch in her throat, then she sighed again, almost with relief, as though she'd been needing him as much as he needed her. That little exhalation made him want to beat his chest and roar, evoking latent cavemen tendencies that he'd never known he'd possessed.

He grasped his arm around the small of her back, scooted her closer to the edge of the table and thrust deeply, wrenching another cry of delight from her.

"God, you feel good," he told her.

"So do you," she said, tightening around him, seemingly trying to hold him inside of her. "I love it when you're here," she meaningfully. "It makes me feel… whole," she finally said, which had not been what he was expecting.

Jackson buried himself to the hilt once more, pistoned in and out of her, savoring every greedy clench and release of her tight little body, relishing every sigh of pleasure. She clung to him, holding him tightly as though she never wanted to let him go and the knowledge that she was as mindless as he was made him weak in the knees.

Her breath caught and a violent tremor shook her body. "Oh, Jack," she whimpered. "I need— I want—"

He reached down between their joined bodies, found her hot-button and pushed it.

Predictably, she shattered.

Her tight heat fisted around him—hard—and her body went rigid with shock, then melted as the pleasure washed over her, taking a little bit of the tension with each pulse of climax.

The phone rang, but neither one of them heeded it.

She wrapped her legs more tightly around him, bent

forward and licked his neck. That one little act was all it took to make Jackson come apart as well. The orgasm blasted from his loins, blackening his vision around the edges, forcing him to lock his legs to keep from hitting the floor. He locked himself tightly inside her, clenched his jaw and made a low growl as the final tremors worked their way through him.

Breathing heavily, he rested his head against hers. "I am...yours to...command," he told her.

Carley chuckled. Her answering machine clicked on, then her recorded voice filled the ensuing silence, eliciting a shared smile.

"Hi, you've reached Carley DeLuna. I'm sorry I can't take your call right now. Please leave a message and I'll get back to you as soon as possible."

"Hey, Carley, it's Abby. Just wanted to check in and see how you were doing. Sam's working on the Carlyle Library project and I've got a new male client—taking a geek to chic," she chuckled. "So anyway, I hate that I missed you. I'll try you again later. In the meantime, don't forget our pact. No nerds, no ditch-diggers and no used-car salesmen. We're better than that."

The silence that followed the final beep of the answering machine thundered between them and, though he knew he shouldn't react, shouldn't lash out, he couldn't seem to help himself. He withdrew from her, stepped back and zipped his pants. The sound seemed to scream between them.

"Jack—"

"You made a pact?" he asked, surprised at just how very much he was hurt. He knew her—he even understood her. But this… There was something too cold-blooded and calculated about it.

"It's not as bad as it sounds," she said, tugging her dress down and sliding off the table.

He didn't see how that could be true. They'd clearly outlined what sort of guy wasn't acceptable, and as a used-car salesman, he definitely didn't make the cut.

"No used-car salesmen, eh?" So that's why she'd looked so disappointed when he'd told her what he was doing for a living now. He'd assumed that she'd just wanted more for him, but clearly she'd just put a big old mental "X" over him as a potential mate. A bitter laugh choked him.

He couldn't do this again, he decided abruptly. She'd thrown him back once before because he hadn't lived up to her standards. Only a fool would let her do it again.

And Jackson Harper was many things, but a fool wasn't one of them.

He turned on his heel, strode to the bedroom and retrieved his bag. Carley followed wordlessly behind him, but seemed to jerk to life when she saw him pick up his overnight case.

"Don't leave, Jack," she said softly. "Let me explain. It was a stupid idea made between bitter women who were striking out in the dating game. I didn't mean—"

"Yeah, it was stupid," he agreed, his mouth dry with regret. "But more than that, it was shallow—" He sent her a look of disappointment. "And frankly, after ten years, I expected better of you."

That dart found its mark, he decided, watching as her eyes widened in hurt. "Jack, don't—"

He shouldered his bag, ignored the immediate knee-jerk instinct to soothe her pain. "You know where I live, Carley. If you ever decide that I'm good enough for you, then look me up."

And without another word, he turned on his heel and left.

CHAPTER NINE

YOU KNOW WHERE I LIVE, Carley. If you ever decide that I'm good enough for you, then look me up.

Rooted to the spot in her bedroom, Carley flinched as she heard the kitchen door close behind Jackson. Her heart pounded sickeningly in her curiously hollow chest and nausea crawled up the back of her throat, forcing her to swallow.

Less than ten minutes ago they'd been making love on her kitchen table and now…

Now he was gone…out of her life.

It was almost surreal, and if she didn't have the achy throb of marathon sex between her legs, if she hadn't felt her chest tighten with the sort of dread and anxiety one might associate with the death of a loved one constricting her breathing, she might have just thought she'd imagined the past couple of days with Jackson.

But she knew better. Her breaking heart told her so.

Carley wished that she could say that he'd jumped to the wrong conclusion about her, wished that she could lay the blame anywhere but at her own feet.

Unfortunately, she knew that wasn't the case. There

was no defending what he'd overheard because it was inexcusable.

Granted there was nothing wrong with her or her friends for wanting a good guy who wouldn't be intimidated by their success. But pigeonholing men simply because of the kind of work that they did was just what he'd said—shallow.

Ashamed, Carley lowered her head and pressed her shaking hands to her face. So long as a guy was gainfully employed and made a girl happy, then what difference did it make?

Jackson had always been a hard worker. And he'd always made her happy. An image of his face burned the backs of her lids.

Gorgeous eyes, sexy smile…and that laugh.

She choked back a sob. Did she wish that he'd gone to college? Yes, but not out of some twisted self-important reason. Education was important, damn it, and he was so damned smart. He would have thrived, he would have loved it.

But it didn't make him any less of man and, more importantly, it didn't make her love him any less because he didn't have a degree.

She felt a watery smile turn her lips. She loved him because he had the singular ability to make her feel like she was the most important person in his world. Only two days back with him and that hadn't changed. He could still stop her heart with a grin, make her tingle with a mere touch of his hand. He was Jackson. Her hero. Her White Knight, her best friend, champion and greatest comfort.

Her soul mate.

And she'd just let him walk out of her life, much the way she had walked out of his ten years ago.

She'd screwed up then, but had absolutely no intention of making the same mistake now. Her gaze slid to her bed and a tear trekked down her cheek, remembering what they'd done, what it had felt like to wake up in those arms this morning.

Melting sighs, skin to skin, moonlight and dawn, redemption and release...

He'd told her that he was hers to command, Carley thought, but she knew that if their relationship was going to work, it was time for her to give up some of that power and let him wield it over her for a change. He'd had the power all along—she'd just never surrendered long enough for him to use it properly.

That was about to change.

"You know where I live," he'd said.

She certainly did, Carley thought, resolved. And thanks to the rental car company, she had a fast car to get her there.

AN HOUR LATER Jackson pulled into his driveway, shifted into Park and gazed out the windshield, not altogether certain why he lingered in his truck.

Unless it was the fact that he'd been fighting the mounting urge to turn right around and head straight back to Charlotte—to Carley, dammit.

He grimly suspected that he'd overreacted.

Of course, that could simply be wishful thinking on his part. Because walking away from her again had felt as if he was tearing his soul in two and he was looking for any excuse to go back.

To be with her.

He knew his own worth, dammit, and he knew that, deep down, she did, too. He loved her enough to do the excavation and wished like hell that he could start immediately.

Unfortunately, he'd put the ball firmly into her court and he had to believe that, in the end, she would toss it back to him. As much as he wanted to go back to her, as much as he needed her, Jackson knew that this was a decision that she needed to make on her own. He had to have faith that she would sort through her feelings for him and ultimately decide that he was worth having, regardless of what sort of job he did.

He needed to know that she knew that as well.

This was for the best, he thought, expelling a breath.

Furthermore, the client he was supposed to see tomorrow had found an unexpected opening in his schedule and had called Jackson's cell phone to see if he could accommodate him. He'd said yes. So even if he wanted to crank his truck back up and point it once again in the direction of Charlotte, he couldn't until after his business was conducted. He was hoping by that time, this incessant urge to go back to her would have waned a little. If not, he was in for a rough rest of his life.

With a resigned sigh, he finally mustered the courage to exit his truck and make his way into the house. Compared to hers, his felt curiously generic, Jackson thought, looking around. Oh, it was nice enough. Spacious, with all the latest modern appliances. Lots of molding and hardwood floors. Rather than do the work himself, he'd hired a decorator who, after realizing Jackson's ambivalence, had simply taken over and done the work without his input. It was his house, but other than the magazines stacked next to the recliner, there was nothing about it that *said* it was his house. It could have been anybody's.

With a start, he'd realized that's what he'd imagined about her and yet he was the one who was guilty. Carley's house was full of character—hers.

Shit, Jackson thought, shoving his hands through his hair. He had to get a grip, had to try and put her out of his mind, at least long enough to sell this damned car.

Speaking of which…

He heard a car pull into the driveway and swore. So the guy was early. He'd hoped to have a minute to warm the motor up and make sure that everything was as it should be before his prospective client arrived, but evidently private planes were swifter transportation than what Jackson was accustomed to.

He barely had time to grab the keys to his shop before there was a knock at his front door. Pasting a professional smile on his face, Jackson opened the door.

Carley.

"Hi," she said, somewhat shyly. "I would have been here sooner, but you were wrong—I, uh…I didn't know where you lived. I had to stop by my parents' apartment and use their phone book to find your address. Then I got lost because it's been s-so long since I was in town and—" She drew up short. "And all of that is pointless, because it's not what I came here to say." She pulled in a bolstering breath. "I came to tell you that I am sorry and that I love you—" Her voice cracked. "I always have and never stopped. And I don't care what you do, so long as it makes you happy. You could drive a garbage truck and I wouldn't give a damn, if that's what you wanted to do."

The chill that had invaded his chest since walking out of her house earlier abruptly fled, chased away by a rush of warm joy that made his insides quake.

"You went by your parents' place?"

She nodded, still looking miserably uncertain. "It was time for a visit. Past time, actually."

So she'd learned that lesson, also, Jackson thought, unbelievably pleased.

Carley fidgeted and gave him a wobbly smile. "Come on, Jack," she said, eyes twinkling. "Gimme something. It's, uh… It's awful lonely out here on this limb."

He laughed. Those were the exact words he'd said to her last night. Jackson sidled forward, wrapped his arms around her waist and looked down at her. "And you don't mind that I'm a used-car salesman? It doesn't bother you that I'm *content*?"

Carley smiled. "Not so long as I can be content with you."

"You're sure?"

"Definitely. I can't lose you again, Jack. I don't think I'd ever get over it."

"In that case, there's probably something I should tell—" He stopped short as a limo pulled into the driveway.

Carley heard it, too, and turned around. She frowned. "Who's that?"

"A client."

"A client?" she parroted, her brow furrowing with confusion.

"I'll explain later," Jackson told her. "Don't leave, okay?"

She glanced from him to the limo, then back to him, her expression piqued with curiosity. She grunted. "Oh, I'm not going anywhere."

Jackson moved past her, jumping off the front steps and meeting his customer by the car. "Good afternoon, sir," he said, offering his hand. "It's good to see you."

"You, too, Mr. Harper." He glanced out toward the shop. "Now let's see this little beauty you've been saving for me."

From the corner of his eye, Jackson watched Carley stroll across the front porch, felt her gaze follow them as he and his client made their way toward his shop. This was going to go one of two ways, he thought. She was either going to be really thrilled or really pissed…and intuition told him to bank on her being the latter.

He hadn't lied, exactly, but he hadn't told her the truth either.

Fifteen minutes and a test drive later, Jackson accepted a hefty check and a handshake. "Pleasure doing business with you, sir," Jackson told the man. "I'll ready the 'vette for shipment and I'll be on the lookout for that '59 Bentley you're looking for."

Evidently Carley had been waiting for Jackson's client to leave, because the instant he climbed back into his limo, she walked into the shop, cast a look around and then shot him a smile.

He wasn't entirely sure he trusted it.

"Was that who I think it was?" she asked.

He nodded. "Probably."

She gestured toward his showroom, at the gleaming antique vehicles positioned there. "And these are the *used* cars you sell?"

Any second now she was going to round on him, Jackson thought. She was entirely too calm. It was making him exceedingly nervous. "They are."

"Vintage?"

He swallowed. "Right."

To his surprise, she laughed and sauntered toward him. Her gaze searched his and she chewed the inside of her cheek. "I guess I deserved that, eh?"

"You leapt to the wrong conclusion," he said, looping his arms around her waist. "I just didn't correct you."

She grinned and licked that spot on his neck that automatically initiated his launch sequence. "Because you are wicked." She let go a little sigh. "Lucky for you I have learned the value of not judging a person's worth by their ambitions…and I'm in the mood for wicked. In fact, I think I may be having an allergic reaction to it. You know, of the intimate sort?"

Jackson felt a chuckle vibrate up his throat. "Just give the command, Brownie and I'll scratch it."

She leaned forward and planted a long, hot kiss upon his lips. "How about *you* give the command and I'll scratch *yours*?"

He drew back, looked down and his gaze tangled with hers. He saw love and hope and happiness and their future reflected back at him and felt a slow smile slide across his lips. "That sounds even better," he said. "You know I love you, right?"

She kissed him again. "I do now."

EPILOGUE

Manhattan
Three months later…

"JUST GOES TO show you," Samantha said with a regal shrug, her light blond hair slipping over her shoulders. "You should never say never."

"That's right," Abby chimed in. "Three months ago we were sitting in this very same café bemoaning the tight market of marriageable men—"

"And limiting our pool by swearing off even more," Carley piped up.

"And now look at us?" Abby finished. Her silver eyes shone with a rare sort of happiness. "We're all in happily-ever-after relationships with the very types of men we said we'd never date."

Samantha's Carlyle Library project had gone off without a hitch and she'd landed more than the patent for her retaining wall system—she'd landed the love of her life, as well.

Abby had set out to make over a nerd—her most

challenging project to date—and had found out that she preferred him as-is, pocket protector and all.

And as for Carley, if she hadn't bought her retro Thunderbird, then it would have never broken down and her used-car salesman couldn't have come along and saved her.

Smiling, Samantha raised her glass. "A toast to irony," she said, her lips curling into a droll smile, "who knocked some much-needed sense into us."

"Hear, hear," Carley said, tucking her hair behind her ears.

Abby clinked her glass against the other two. "To ditch-diggers."

Carley grinned. "And geeks."

"And used-car salesmen," Samantha added. "Honestly, if I had known making that ridiculous pact was going to bring the right men out of the woodwork, you can bet we would have done it sooner."

"Better late than never, though," Abby said with a soft sigh.

"Amen to that, sister." Samantha and Carley agreed.

**Introducing an exciting appearance
by legendary
New York Times bestselling author**

DIANA PALMER

HEARTBREAKER

He's the ultimate bachelor...
but he may have just met
the one woman to change his ways!

Join the drama in the story of a confirmed
bachelor, an amnesiac beauty and their
unexpected passionate romance.

**"Diana Palmer is a mesmerizing storyteller
who captures the essence of what
a romance should be."—*Affaire de Coeur***

**Heartbreaker *is available from Silhouette Desire
in September 2006.***

Silhouette®

SPECIAL EDITION™

Experience the "magic" of falling in love at Halloween with a new *Holiday Hearts* story!

UNDER HIS SPELL

by KRISTIN HARDY

October 2006

Bad-boy ski racer J. J. Cooper can get any woman he wants—except Lainie Trask. Lainie's grown up with him and vows that nothing he says or does will change her mind. But J.J.'s got his eye on Lainie, and when he moves into her neighborhood and into her life, she finds herself falling under his spell....

HOLIDAY HEARTS

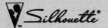